DEADLY OBJECTIVES

L. A. Taylor

"A new addition to the ranks of top-notch suspense authors."

Minneapolis Star

J. J. Jamison is an affable young computer engineer – hardly a detective – but he and his Danish office mate are delegated to track down a piece of secret equipment that has disappeared. That's when the trouble begins . . . the equipment reappears and Jamison's wife and son now disappear . . . maybe kidnapped. He also has to find a con man who's involved with UFO's. A couple of murders and other dramatic events complicate matters but J.J. manages to come up with a novel and exciting resolution.

Deadly Objectives

L. A. TAYLOR

John Curley & Associates, Inc.
South Yarmouth, Ma.

Library of Congress Cataloging in Publication Data

Taylor, Laurie
Deadly objectives.

1. Large type books. I. Title.
[PS3570.A943D4 1986] 813′.54 86–434
ISBN 1–55504–093–4 (lg. print)
ISBN 1–55504–104–3 (soft : lg. print)

Published in Large Print by arrangement with Walker & Company in the U.S.A. and Sally Gouverneur & Company for the U.K. and Commonwealth.

Distributed in the U.K. and Commonwealth by Magna Print Books.

Printed in Great Britain

The places in this book are, except in some details, real places. The people are not, and none of their actions are based upon the deeds or misdeeds of any real person.

DEADLY OBJECTIVES

First

The line jerked forward one notch.

Another pair of shoulders in a London Fog raincoat blocked the ticket desk; along the line anxious glances bounded from watch dials to the blue-gray stare of the television screen behind the counter. The agent's questions, dull with the early hour, rose into the height of the terminal and diffused among a row of listless flags. Somewhere a child's crying echoed; the occasional scrape of a shoe sharpened the air; once every few minutes heavy engines rumbled outside, oddly unnoticed.

The line moved again. Three back from the desk, now, a thirtyish man whose coat flapped open over a plaid jacket and a rumpled tie dotted with small green fish shoved a black case forward to fill the opening space.

The case came almost to his knees and could have contained, say, a musical instrument; but the logo slapped on each side of the case belonged to a computer firm, not an orchestra. Under the words "return to" someone had applied a bright green Mr. Yuk sticker.

The man rested his carry-on case on top of the black one and folded his arms. The television screen blinked. As the list of flights shifted upward a small spasm ran through the waiting group. The man glanced at his watch, noticed that his tie was rucked up and straightened it, tapped his foot.

The London Fog at the head of the line peeled away and dashed for the Blue Concourse. The rest of the line jerked forward again.

When the man with the black case reached the desk, he pulled a sheaf of traveler's checks out of an inner pocket and slapped it down. "Two to Los Angleles," he said, starting to sign a check. "One for me and one for my friend, here."

"I'm sorry, sir. You can't take that on the airplane with you," the ticket agent said.

"Not even with a ticket?"

"Sorry, no. Not if it's too big to fit under the seat." The agent peered across the desk at the man's signature. "Mr. Chapin, is it? It's a matter of passenger safety. The, uh, thing has to be well-secured, and we can't guarantee that the seat belt will do it. In case of turbulence, you know." The agent fetched a grin out of his Thursday-morning blahs and pasted it around his teeth. "We wouldn't want it bouncing all over the cabin, would we?"

"I've seen a cello," Chapin protested.

"On another airline, maybe." The man's eyes flicked toward the next person in line.

"Can I check it through?" Chapin asked hastily. "Do you have something like special handling?"

"We can arrange something."

"One to L.A., then, and check my friend through."

"Is he - ah, it - very heavy?"

"Oh, no." Chapin tore out a traveler's check and handed it across the counter. "Forty pounds at the outside." He boosted the case onto the scale at his feet. "Take care of her, though, she's an expensive lady."

"Yes, sir." The man glanced at Chapin as if wondering whether he were dealing with a trunk murderer, shrugged, and began writing out the ticket. He finished just as Chapin tore out the last of the checks needed to cover the fare. He scribbled on a tag and looped it over the handle of the case, stapled the stub of the tag to the ticket envelope with a final-sounding *clunk,* and counted out change. "Have a nice flight," he grunted as he swung the case onto the conveyor belt behind him.

"Thanks." Chapin picked up his overnight case, slipped past the man crowding up to the counter behind him, and headed for the Blue Concourse at a brisk trot.

Six hours later and fifteen hundred miles away, he gave up waiting for the black case to come through the baggage claim area and hunted up someone in a uniform to ask about it.

"Gee, I dunno." The girl he'd found fixed her eyes on the tie with the green fish and blinked. "Maybe in the special baggage section?"

"Thanks."

"Have-a-nice-day," she enjoined.

Still hoping for a nice day, Chaplin checked the boxes and bags on the special baggage cart, one of which meowed at him, and then the larger items in the special baggage room, three of which barked at him.

The black case wasn't in either place. He hung around for another hour, but still it didn't show up. Then, no longer just annoyed, he rubbed his tongue against the roof of his mouth to moisten it and went in search of a telephone.

Chapter One

"He did *what?*"

"He lost it," Pedersen repeated. The blood drained out of my face and collected in a cold clump in my stomach.

"How? When?"

Pedersen leaned back in his swivel chair and folded his arms behind his head. Very slowly a broad smile opened his long face. "How? That, Jamison, is precisely what everyone would like to know." The chair squeaked once to underscore the grin. "When? While you were wasting your time chasing flying what's-its in North Dakota."

Wasting time, right. Four of my precious vacation days – six days total, with the weekend – just to hand out half a dozen or so of the cards that identify me as Joseph Jamison, field investigator for the Committee for Analysis of Tropospheric and Celestial Happenings, usually called CATCH. As usual, the reported UFO had turned out to be nothing spectacular: just three large, helium-filled Mylar balloons, the kind I could have bought for my young son at any local shopping center without driving twelve hundred miles in a balky 1978 Ford. For that matter, I could have sat home in comfort and ordered them ten at a time, complete with helium tank, from Edmund Scientific, which is what the kid in Bottineau, *north* North Dakota, had done. The six days, even discounting the monotony of prairie driving, would obviously have been a lot livelier if I'd spent them at work.

Well, with school back in session after the Christmas holidays, at least the UFO season would settle back into its winter slough. "You'd better tell me about it," I sighed, prepared for a typical Pedersen lecture.

"That's it."

"What do you mean, that's it? Did Aunt Yuk vaporize, or what?"

I'm not sure where Aunt Yuk got her nickname. Burns, my boss, or maybe Kochel, his boss, gave it to her. She's an experimental pattern recognizer we built on a commercial contract: feed her a snapshot of Cousin Charlie and she'll prepare it for storage in the computer of your choice. Then show her a picture of a crowd with Cousin Charlie in it, give her the run of the computer, and she'll pick him out about fifty times faster than his own mother could. The gadget can be used for many other purposes, of course – the FBI was dickering with the company for one to sort fingerprints, just as soon as we worked all the bugs out – and the Department of Defense had taken a belated interest in it.

"Chapin was escorting the prototype to Los Angeles," Pedersen relented. "He couldn't coax the ticket agent into selling him a seat for her" – knowing Chapin, I didn't think he'd tried very hard – "so she had to go below with the luggage. At least, I think that's what happened. I spoke with Chapin yesterday, but he sounded perhaps hysterical, saying peculiar things about baggage that barked and meowed."

"Dogs and cats," I theorized. "They travel with the baggage."

"Oh, that is good to hear. I had feared he was losing his sanity, which I thought rather an overreaction, even in the circumstances. All he can say is that he decided to check the case through, the flight was direct, and when he got to California, the case was no longer on the airplane."

"They bombed Denver with her, or what?"

"That, Jamison, is what we must discover."

The remark didn't register. If I thought about it at all, I probably took him to mean "we" as the company we work for, a company that had sunk over $8,000,000 in development into that prototype. I was stunned, and for all his nonchalance, Pedersen must have been, too: two years of our professional lives had just gone up in smoke. Pedersen's, even more than mine: he was the software lead for the project, meaning that his was the basic design. But I, as an engineer, had done a good deal of the detail work.

"Kidnapped?" I hazarded, when Pedersen failed to continue.

"Who knows?" Pedersen's chair came forward with a crash and his bony hands slapped his knees. "And now, may I suggest that you call your stockbroker immediately and sell every last share you have in this company before the rumor spreads. Then we can go to the airport."

I glanced at the telephone. "Are we fleeing the country?"

"Oh, my dear Jamison, heaven forfend! I am sure it won't come to such an extremity." Pedersen favored me with his blandest look. Scandinavian that he is, it resembles sweet butter. "No, we are simply seeking to begin our investigation where the object in question was last reliably observed."

"*Our* investigation?"

Pedersen cast patient blue eyes toward the

ceiling. "Did I not, only moments ago, inform you that we are to discover what has happened to our dear Aunt Yuk?" he inquired.

"Us?"

"Don't squeak, Jamison. It detracts from whatever air of authority you may possess. We'll need to exhibit some credibility if we are to succeed in extracting the requisite information from persons who may or may not be disposed toward cooperation."

"Lars," I said, with a pang of suspicion. "Are you putting me on?"

"Alas, no."

I stared at him. He looked perfectly serious. Not that that means anything with Pedersen. "You're sure this isn't your idea of a joke? The whole thing?"

"No joke," he sighed. "The pattern discriminator has disappeared, and yes, the job of finding it has been assigned to us." With a face that innocent, nobody would ever guess that the man has a wife and six kids and a mortgage, and access at will to just about any information in any computer system in the country, as long as there's a telephone line into it.

"Why us?"

"Read your mail. That is how people find out what they are supposed to be doing."

I reached for the stack of memos that had accumulated since the Wednesday before. "One question. Does anyone outside the company know about this? The customer, for instance?"

"I sincerely hope not. Read your mail."

I skipped phoning my broker, since I'd sold all my company stock three months earlier, just before its price rose so steeply that it made headlines in the *Wall Street Journal,* and leafed through my mail. Sure enough, there was a pink *urgent* memo from R. Quentin Burns asking me to aid Lars Pedersen in a "very, very confidential" investigation into the straying of Aunt Yuk, a job for which he supposed me to be qualified because of my "experience as an investigator," "the need for absolute secrecy," and my "familiarity with the object sought." What he didn't have to say was that penalties of thousands of dollars a day would be assessed against the company if we missed out delivery deadline, and that building another prototype in the time we had was impossible.

R. Quentin Burns happens to have been manager of my unit for the past five years: my boss. Not even Pedersen could forge a signature like a trough of spaghetti. So that was that.

Chapter Two

Industrial espionage; one company stealing the manufacturing secrets of another, to avoid the huge costs of developing a similar product on its own.

That kind of spying is the terror of most technological companies, although the general public hears of it only in scattered cases – for instance, when the Japanese tried to "steal" an IBM computer. IBM is a good example of the lengths to which some companies go to guard their products, whether Uncle Sam considers them secret or not. Even the company telephone directory is confidential: you can get yourself fired for taking one home. Security guards there don't just rattle the locks, I've heard. I don't know it it's true, but I'm told they check desks at night to see if you've left any papers sitting out – and they take whatever papers they find away with them, so you can only get them back from your boss. Bosses at IBM have a reputation for sternness. Imagine trying to explain away your football pool slips on a hungover Monday morning, if you will – to say nothing of mere top-secret work left lying around.

My own company isn't nearly as big as IBM, and consequently isn't nearly as paranoid. You can't get past the guard desk at the door without some kind of pass, true, but the passes aren't that hard to get. Even a wife picking her husband up after work can get one, if she's accompanied by a small child dancing-desperate to get to the john. Oh, a couple of places in the plant are closed, like the hardware shop where Aunt Yuk was built: those you can't get into without a special personal ID, read by a laser to unlock the door, exactly the way some supermarkets read Universal Product Codes. In this case the merchandise also has to know the correct numbers to punch into the buttons to unlock the second door, or it still can't check out. Neither of these little hitches would give any trouble to a guy like Pedersen (who can play any computer as adroitly as Isaac Stern plays the violin, and make it sing as well), but for the rest of us pedestrian types, they're effective enough. Not that I'm saying Pedersen ever tried to visit where he wasn't welcome. I don't know and I don't want to know.

Outside the plant, if it's impractical to hire guards with snazzy uniforms and an armored car, we rely on what I call the PLA, for Purloined Letter Approach, after Poe's story about a compromising letter "hidden" just by putting it in a desk among other letters. Like sending Aunt Yuk to Los Angeles on an ordinary flight - which is what got her into trouble.

Pedersen had folded his long limbs into the driver's seat of his Volvo and driven through assorted red, amber, and green traffic lights with proportionately increasing speed and decreasing caution, and I was clutching the bucket seat beside him. "Who knew Chapin would be on that flight?" I asked, as he wheeled his buggy onto 35W.

"According to R. Quentin, only our group even knew *when* he was going." Pedersen glanced over his shoulder and dovetailed the Volvo between a bus and a semi. He settled back to steer with his usual two fingers, leaving a hand free for punctuation. "That is official. But the secretary must have known the day before that he was leaving, because she had to get him his traveler's checks." He looked at me. I looked at the road. "Has it ever struck you, Jamison, that secretaries are invisible people? No?" I relaxed by .005 on a scale of 1 to 10 as he glanced at the road ahead. "The ticket had to be bought at the airport just before he left, reservations being thought an unnecessary frill by this airline.

"Unofficially, since we've had a memo directing us to use a specific airline, and since that airline has precisely one flight to Los Angeles on Thursdays, the necessary deduction is not of a prohibitive order of difficulty," Pedersen pointed out. "Not even for Lisa." Lisa's the secretary, a cheery girl and a speedy typist, but solidly at the bottom of the average stanine for intelligence. "Once the flight was underway, if Chapin had not called to say that something had gone wrong – and of course he didn't, since he didn't know yet that it had – R. Quentin was to call the Los Angeles office to let them know Aunt Yuk was coming. Which he did. I happened to overhear Lisa placing a call to Los Angeles, myself."

Pedersen swung out to pass a truck just as I thought he was about to run under it. "Why didn't Chapin keep the thing with him?" I asked, just as if I could think.

"I gather the ticket salesman had some trifling prejudice against it. Perhaps he thought it looked dangerous."

"Chapin could have said it was a musical instrument."

Pedersen gave me a lingering glance that riveted my eyes to the road whizzing under the Volvo's wheels. The highway was midmorning bare, and the Volvo has excellent seat belts, but Pedersen can't read speed limit signs and one of us had to watch what traffic there was. "It's difficult to imagine the sort of creature that might play the instrument that would fit into a case of that shape," he observed. "Perhaps that's something you'll discover, when one of these objects you investigate turns out to be of extraterrestrial origin."

"Lars, for God's sake, you're doing over eighty!"

"Kilometers, Jamison. So Chapin, impetuous youth that he is, decided to check the case through, rather than risk the wrath of R. Quentin – it wouldn't fit under the seat, and his instructions were not to miss that flight under any circumstances."

"How come the speedometer's marked *mph* if it's in kilometers?"

Pedersen flicked the fingers on his right hand as if getting rid of a particularly pestiferous fly, but he did slow down to sixty-five. I eyed the snow banked beside the road and wondered how much energy it would absorb if Pedersen hit it. "Therefore we will attempt to trace the path of the case," Pedersen said, tranquil as he'd been in his swivel chair. "I've taken the liberty of calling the president of the airline Chapin traveled on –"

"Am I allowed to know which one, or is that secret, too?"

The Volvo swayed on its springs as Pedersen made the shift from 35W to the Crosstown. "Budjetair," he said. "B-U-D-J-E-T-A-I-R."

"Never heard of them."

"Read your mail, Jamison, as I advised you earlier this morning. Burns decided last week that a smaller and less costly airline would be more appropriate for travels of the sort Aunt Yuk was scheduled to make, as there would be less chance of observation and hence of something untoward occurring."

"Wrong."

"Obviously."

The route Pedersen was taking circles around the east end of the airport, and a large, low, very loud aircraft passed over our heads just then. The interior of the car blinked in its shadow. "At any rate," Pedersen shouted, "we will interview this man and see what, if anything, we can discover."

As good a place to start as any, I figured. Unless, of course, the president of Budjetair was given to swiping miscellaneous pieces of electronic equipment on speculation, a possibility so remote it made me wonder about my own paranoia just because I'd thought of it.

Signs for the airport appeared as we rounded the next curve. I wondered what Pedersen's sometimes mischievous sense of humor might lead him to say to the president of Budjetair, and whether I wanted to be present when he said it. I don't have much taste for squirming in my seat. "Do you know where to go?" I asked, as we wheeled into the approach road and charged past the low yellowish buildings labeled *Western*, an airline I *had* heard of.

"Of course."

Ten minutes of twisting and turning through airport roads made me wonder about Pedersen's command of the English language. *Of course?* Then he braked, hard, just in time to avoid crashing into a brick wall. The wall had a door in it, and above the door was a sign saying BUDJETAIR in black block letters on a white board. "What do you know, a generic airline," I said, and released the seat belt.

Inside the door, the airline looked less generic than shabby. The dreary, off-white room held only three plastic chairs and a desk, on which a bell sat beside a sign that promised service if it were rung. Pedersen achieved an act of faith and rang it.

"Think we could sue them for the eight million?" I asked.

"They'd have to sell their airplane."

"They've only got one?" I exclaimed.

"Actually, I think they have three."

A woman, not at all shabby, especially around the chest and ankles, opened an inner door and asked what we wanted. Pedersen explained. Her smile vanished as if it had been sucked in. "Mr. Devitt will see you right away," she said.

The budget theme continued into the president's office, where some Astroturf had died on the floor, right on up to the desk. The desk announced that the buck stopped there. Judging by Basil Devitt's tailoring, that's just what it did.

He had nothing to tell us, but it took a long time to be told: Pedersen inquired about the case (still missing), assured Mr. Basil Devitt that yes, Chapin had a receipt, and got a rundown on baggage-handling procedure. Pedersen, being Pedersen, extended the agony to learn that baggage tags are color coded, which he should have known, that they have the airline's name on them and the flight number written in, which I could have told him, and that there was simply no possibility of error. I tried not to yawn.

"Do the bags always travel on the same plane as the passenger?" Pedersen asked.

"Almost always," Devitt said. He was having trouble not yawning himself. "If the bags are checked late, or we have an overflow for some reason, we may put something on another flight. One of the larger airlines can usually accommodate us. But in that case, the passenger would be told."

"And in this case?"

"Didn't happen. I checked. And it's not still in the airplane – I checked that, too. Personally."

But Pedersen was just getting started. By the time we left, he'd goaded Devitt nearly to the explosion point. On the way out, he lit up his blue eyes and wide smile for the secretary-receptionist, but she only produced a smile to match. No black case.

"All the same," Pedersen said as he unlocked the car, "I think we'll go have a look at the ticket desk for Budjetair."

Budjetair, we discovered after passing through the gate into the parking ramp and depositing the Volvo for a minimum charge of one buck, sold tickets only during the hour before a flight. The no-reservations policy was one of the so-called airline's so-called attractions; all of its planes were headed out and the single station assigned to the company was empty. The belt with luggage aimed for the bellies of planes belonging to more fortunate airlines rumbled along behind Budjetair's place just as if it didn't exist.

Pedersen stared at it and pulled his chin, turning his head to look toward the Blue Concourse. "Let's have some coffee," he suggested at last. "As long as we're here."

"Sounds good."

"I'll even buy. We have an expense account, did you know?"

I didn't, and I was startled. R. Quentin's faith in us – or his fear of the head office – must be stronger than I had thought. Pedersen led the way from the broad, cool, open space of the terminal into the closer, warmer, noisier coffee shop and got into the short line. "Has R. Quentin been in touch with Kochel?" I asked.

"I don't know," Pedersen admitted. "I imagine not, don't you? Kochel's warming his bones in the Caribbean for another two weeks, and it would be a real coup if Burns could handle this himself and present the results to his boss."

"Mmm." Must be nice to leapfrog through the promotions the way Kochel has, I was thinking. He'd been with the company six years, and was already senior to men who had been with them three times as long.

We settled at one of the smaller tables with coffee, the quality a welcome relief from the slop we'd have been drinking out of the vending machine at work. Pedersen examined his pastry closely and grumbled about its being called Danish.

"Are you thinking what I'm thinking?" I asked.

"Highly unlikely." Pedersen sipped at his coffee and grimaced. "Do you care to enlighten me?"

"I think somebody stole Aunt Yuk."

He glanced at me, eyelids lowered to conceal his amusement. A considerate man at times, Pedersen. "Reasonable conclusion," he pronounced. "Do you propose a course of action based upon that assumption?"

"No," I sighed. "I just came in, remember? You've had, what, a whole weekend and a Monday to live with it."

"I didn't give it a thought over the weekend," Pedersen said. "Margritte had an ear infection. So it's only a two-day start I have, really. Counting Friday."

I opened my mouth to say something about the subconscious workings of the normal mind, and so forth, but there's no point in arguing with the Great Dane, as my wife calls him, so I shut my mouth on the sweet roll I'd chosen.

"I'm exceedingly curious," said Pedersen.

"That's a help."

"Not about our problem. About that man at the corner table."

"What about him?" Somehow I'd managed to choose a bun with raisins in it. I loathe raisins. I began picking them out of the bun.

"He skulks."

"Skulks?"

"That is the correct word, is it not?" Pedersen asked, his forehead screwed into lines. "Meaning, 'to move furtively'?"

"Yeah, I guess. What do you mean, he skulks?"

"While we were searching for the ticket desk, and while we examined its desolation, I noticed that he ducked to the other side of the information booth in the center of the floor and peeked out at us. When he ran into the coffee shop, I was inspired to follow."

I might have known there was more to it than a sudden insatiable desire for coffee.

"Then, when we came in, he stared at us as we went through the line. When we sat down, he shifted his seat so that his back is toward us. Now, why do you suppose he did that?"

"Maybe he thinks you've got Auntie in your shirt pocket and he's waiting for a chance to rip her off." I took what looked like a clear bite and got a raisin stuck on my back teeth.

"Yes, we could be being followed," Pedersen said judiciously. "Isn't that surveillance? I can't imagine quite why anyone would want to – is *hold us under* correct usage with surveillance?"

"You're asking me?" I asked, muffled by my finger trying to peel the gook off my tooth.

Pedersen shook his head and made a tsking sound. "Does he look at all familiar to you, Jamison?"

I examined the man he nodded at. The guy was on the tall side, even sitting, was wearing a plaid flannel shirt and jeans, and had very ordinary brown hair in a very ordinary haircut getting shaggy at the back. The stems of glasses showed behind his ears. I shrugged. "If he's a secret agent, he picked a good disguise."

"Well." Pedersen put on his bland look and slathered butter on his not-Danish. "Perhaps nothing."

We finished our break with one of those dark clouds labeled "gloom" hanging over our table. I don't know what Pedersen was thinking, but I was manufacturing a dark scenario involving an interview with R. Quentin Burns in which Pedersen and I admitted an early defeat. Pedersen leaned back with his coffee cup near his mouth: not drinking, just holding it there. I was sure he'd emptied it just after finishing his roll, and I couldn't imagine what he was doing. Whatever it was, it made me nervous.

Plaid Shirt got up and stuck a hand into the pocket of his jeans. Pedersen put the cup down.

Plaid Shirt collected an olive-drab coat from one of the other chairs at his table and hurried out of the coffee shop. Pedersen got up and followed at a leisurely pace. I sorted through my change for a tip and caught up with him a moment later.

"What's up?"

Pedersen grinned and pointed with his chin.

Charles Lindbergh's first airplane had gone on display in the main terminal building a few weeks earlier, suspended from the ceiling as if in flight. Beneath it was the skeleton of another, similar biplane, surrounded on one end by a phalanx of explanatory posters mounted on tall plywood panels. Plaid Shirt almost sprinted for the display and circled behind the plywood wall. "See?"

Pedersen asked. I didn't trust the gleam in his eye.

"See what?"

Plaid Shirt, now transformed into Olive-drab Coat, peered out from behind a large poster. "Now, what is he doing?" Pedersen mused. "I think he is looking for us, don't you?"

"What for?"

"Who knows?" Pedersen sauntered toward the nearest exit. "Maybe we can entice him into revealing his interest," he said. With all my self-protective instincts screaming, I stayed beside him.

"Take a look at our friend." I did as instructed: Olive-drab Coat was just coming around the nose end of the Jenny display.

"He's coming out, if that's what you want to know." At least the joke wasn't going to be on me. I hoped.

"Mmmm."

I took it that I was supposed to be quiet. Olive-drab Coat, I saw out of the tail of my eye, was heading for the next exit over, with many glances in our direction. He did look a little familiar, I realized. Something about the way he moved. Yes, I might have seen him before. Not recently, I was sure of that, so if he was following us it hadn't been for long, but where had I seen him?

Some Saturday afternoon at the movies when I was a kid, I decided. The Indian creeping up on the wagon train.

Pedersen slipped through the nearest exit, almost bowling over a sable-swathed old lady on teetery heels, and dashed for the door his quarry had used. I pounded after him. We arrived just as Olive-drab Coat emerged from the sliding doors.

"The investigation will continue," Pedersen said into the man's face, and turned and tugged on my arm. Bewildered, I shambled after him. A little dry noise came out of Pedersen, growing slowly louder. Pedersen was chuckling.

"What in hell was that about?" I demanded.

"Who was it that said that if you go to a man on the street and say, 'Fly, all is discovered,' nine out of ten will leave town on the next available conveyance?"

"You're asking me?"

"He'll stay clear of us now." Pedersen chuckled.

"Stay clear! He wasn't anywhere near us! You know, one of these days your sense of humor is going to get you in deep trouble."

Trouble arrived right on cue, flapping her furs and hissing like a teakettle with laryngitis. "You, do you know you're a menace to society?" she shrieked, catching Pedersen's sleeve in her red-polished claws. "People like you should be locked up until they learn some manners!"

Chuckling myself, I left Pedersen to deal with the elderly Fury and escaped into the parking ramp, where he had left the Volvo. The weather, although warm for a Minnesota January, was fairly cold, but even so I was just as happy to lean against the car with my fists in my pockets until he had smoothed down the old lady's fur. Took him ten minutes. Pedersen was losing his touch.

He came grinning up to the car with the keys in his hand. "Too much time wasted, maybe," he said, getting in.

I refrained from agreeing and waited for him to reach across to open my door. He was chuckling again when I climbed in. The Volvo instantly sped backward in a tight curve. "Oh, well, it was worth it," Pedersen said, standing on the brake. "Did you see his expression?"

Expression! I'd barely had time to see his face! Round, light-rimmed glasses over eyes so pale they looked silver. I knew I'd never seen eyes like that before. A long face with a square jaw, brown hair that fell over a narrow forehead. Still vaguely familiar, like someone I might see once in a while at the other end of a corridor in the plant.

I buckled my seat belt as Pedersen careened around the curves of the exit ramp, and wondered if we would live long enough to put the coffee on our new expense account. To say nothing of my tip.

Chapter Three

The *R.* of R. Quentin Burns stands for Robert. We call the man Bob to his face, but he's as unpoetic a man as ever lived and not even a Scot, so he feels honor bound to sign his name on the principle of least confusion. I wasn't even calling him "Bob" on that afternoon: the atmosphere in his office had begun to resemble the parking lot outside his window, where the first heavy snow of the winter had been shoved into mounds that would grow into mountains by spring. I had decided to let Pedersen do the talking.

Burns is another of those tallish, thinish men the electronics field seems to attract, with enough fat on him to push his shirt over his belt a bit at the sides. Older than either me or Pedersen, he had gray spreading from the temples across his dark hair, and in the past year or so he had developed pouches under his eyes and lines from cheekbones to jaw that accentuated his present unhappiness.

"It looks as if we'll have to call in ARA," he said. The corners of his mouth collapsed downward. "I hate to do it, but the man is supposed to be very discreet, and that's what we need."

My curiosity got the better of my resolve to keep quiet. "What's ARA?"

"ARA? They're a sort of detective agency specializing in industrial espionage cases. Where you don't want to call in the cops, you know, like if the rest of the world hears about your problem everybody and his uncle sells your stock short and makes a bundle." R. Quentin sighed. I remembered Pedersen's advice and wondered if my boss had sold his company stock short. Knowing Burns, I thought not.

"Headquarters has already suggested calling them in." R. Quentin continued. "Him in. It's really a one-man operation, but very good, very smooth. We've used him before." He paused and grimaced. "Never on anything as big as this, though."

"If you don't trust us –" Pedersen began.

"It's not a matter of trust." Burns made a swift gesture like a symphony conductor calling for more decrescendo. "It's that ARA is in Los Angeles, and you two are here with other things to do, and this end doesn't look as if it will pan out."

Whatever he said was fine with me. I didn't join in Pedersen's plea that we'd only just started. I had plenty to do without chasing spies, and while Pedersen might be bored enough to want a break, I liked my job and had some catching up to do.

"Oh, all right," Burns snapped. "Do what you want, as long as you get your other stuff done. Maybe you'll luck out."

I spent the afternoon on things that had piled up while I was chasing balloons along the Canadian border, and went home.

"Guess what," I said to Karen, who was fishing green beans out of a pot with a slotted spoon. "Remember Bill Chapin?"

"The guy that spent four years installing a new bathroom? Gave a kegger the day he got the toilet in?"

"That's him." I took the dish of beans out of her hands and put it on the kitchen table. Joey stood up in his high chair and reached for the beans. I moved the dish farther away. "He's got himself in hot water."

"Good for him," she said. "Cold showers in this weather could kill an Eskimo."

"That's not it. He got tired of creative plumbing and moved into an apartment last summer. I mean, he's in trouble."

"Really?" Karen took a soufflé from the oven and set it on a hot pad in the center of the table, where it hissed and crackled as it prepared to collapse.

"He lost Aunt Yuk."

That got her attention. "He *lost* it? How? When? Where?"

"How, is anybody's guess. It seems to have evaporated in midair on the way to Los Angeles. When, last Thursday. And if I could tell you where, I might get a bonus that would put a deck on the back of the house and finish off an office in the basement for each of us."

"With locks?"

"Steel walls, if you want." I helped myself to soufflé and it finished caving in.

Karen cast a look of longing at Joey, aged eighteen months. Only the day before he had given her brand-new electronic typewriter a treatment of blackberry jam mixed with sand from the box I had rashly brought into the basement for winter play. "You won't, of course," she sighed.

"No. They're turning the investigation over to some outfit in California. Lars and I had a go at it this morning, but all we did was shake up some guy who looks like the male half of a Barbie doll."

"Ken," my wife supplied. "What on earth were you two doing in it?"

"Beats me. Bob Burns thought we could help."

"Typical." Karen shook her head. "No wonder the man's still a unit manager." She put a spoonful of beans on Joey's plate, and I watched for a moment as he pursued one with the end of his spoon, gave up, and delicately ate it with his fingers.

"S'atta, Da?" he asked, opening his brown eyes wide.

"Nothing," Karen said for me. To me, she said, "I hope that's as far as it goes. I'm sick to death of investigations."

"The others were for CATCH."

"I know." She shrugged unhappily and pursued some beans of her own with her fork, her shoulders slumped.

"S'atta, Mommy?" Joey asked.

"Nothing." Karen looked up at me and served herself and Joey some soufflé with a little shake, as if she had forgotten all about it.

"What is the matter, Kay?"

"Oh, I don't know. I know it's important to you. CATCH, that is." She stopped talking again and steadied Joey's plate on the tray for him.

I ate four or five forkfuls of soufflé: hot and cheesy and delicious, as always, a rare, cholesterol-laden treat from Karen, who likes to take charge of my waist and arteries. She still said nothing, although most evenings she chatters about her day, about Joey's latest accomplishments, about the birds in the feeder she can see out the back window, about the writing she's trying to do while Joey naps.

"Karen?" I prompted.

"I'm sorry." Her words were muffled. "We'll talk about it when Joey's in bed."

So I was left in suspense while we finished dinner – Karen forgot to dress the salad, a sure sign that she was upset – and loaded the dishwasher and cleaned up our son without even the usual joke about tossing him in with the dishes. I read Joey a story while Karen made coffee, and then, with our son salted away for the night (with any luck), Karen and I sat facing each other from the ends of the couch in the family room. "And?" I said.

"And." She sipped at the coffee, put the cup on the end table, and stared at it. I began to get scared: Karen doesn't often find it hard to talk. Wild thoughts had been chasing through my head since dinner: someone I knew had died. Something was wrong with Joey. Now a new one: a lump in one of Karen's soft, rounded breasts.

"It's CATCH," she sighed. "I – oh, Joe, I know it means a lot to you, and it was even a lot of fun for me before Joey was born and I could go along on some of the trips, but –"

The Committee for Analysis of Tropospheric and Celestial Happenings. A weird name for a not terribly weird organization, chosen to make the acronym spell "catch," because that was the general idea: to catch a UFO – or at least to prove that they do or do not exist. I'd uncovered more hoaxes than I could remember, tried to give an easy letdown to dozens of sober citizens who'd mistaken Venus or weather balloons or seagulls or advertising planes for extraterrestrial visitors, fended off kooks by the carload, and two or three times I'd come across something I still didn't understand. I'd never caught a saucer: that would have made headlines in the *National Enquirer*, and maybe even in the *New York Times*. Failure didn't bother me. What I liked was the chase. Not fun, exactly. A release, maybe, from the strict logic of my job.

"Now –" Karen continued, stiff-voiced. "Now, like this last trip – you know you used up all but one day of your vacation time, messing around in North Dakota? In January! All that driving! I was scared to death the car would break down or there'd be a blizzard and you'd freeze –"

"You could have come with me."

"Six days on the road with a kid just starting toilet training?" She got up and went into the kitchen for the coffee pot. She had a point.

"But that's not all," she said, coming back and pouring into my cup, as always. "It's – I thought we were saving that time to go on a winter vacation, maybe go visit my folks. But we can't go anywhere now, not with just one day left."

I clasped my hands between my knees. "What do you want me to do?"

"Give it up."

I blinked at her.

"Oh, all right, maybe not all of it, but give up some of it. At least the traveling part. Maybe if you just took the metro area . . ."

"Not much happens here."

"Enough." She was tart about it, with reason: the last time I'd poked into a hoax in the Cities I'd ended up in the middle of a bunch of murders and only missed being burned to a crisp because Joey chose that particular night to be born. Karen wasn't looking at me, just into her cup, her face in shadow and an aureole of back-lit curls around her head. Her knees were drawn up, one sock-covered foot tucked under the other, making a denim wall of her jeans.

"Well," she sighed. "Think about it, will you?"

"OK."

"I mean it," she snapped. "Really. Seriously. Because when you're gone, especially since that – that other time, you've got no idea what it's like for me! Every little noise sounds like somebody breaking in, I don't get to sleep for hours, and then Joey's up at six – I bet I didn't get more than four hours' sleep a night the whole time. By Sunday I was about having hallucinations."

"You need a dog."

"No, I don't need a dog," she said, in a tone that suggested that she thought she might already have one. "I need you." She tipped up her cup to drain it and put it down on the coffee table. Something was missing, I realized: all the bright pamphlets of things to do in Florida, where her parents lived, had disappeared while I was gone. Karen had stopped daydreaming about a vacation for the three of us, because I'd used up all our time driving over miles of wind-haunted prairie, all by myself.

"Karen, I'm sorry," I said.

"Every time the wind blows, the damn house creaks – oh, well. Forget it." Karen got up and took both cups into the kitchen. I head them clink into the sink and the refrigerator door open and shut as she put something away. "Anything on TV to-night?" she called.

"I don't know," I said. "I'll check."

Ten seconds later, the telephone rang. If it had been Prunella Watson calling from CATCH headquarters with another sighting to check, I might have resigned on the spot. But it wasn't. Just a wrong number, some guy with an age-cracked voice wanting to know if Sam would be home later tonight.

I told him I didn't know and hung up.

Chapter Four

I handed Pedersen one cup of the coffee I'd beaten the nearest vending machine into giving up and sat down at my desk with my own. He set the plastic cup, as usual, on one of the back corners of his desk. It was a minute or two before I realized that he hadn't gone back to work, but had swiveled his chair around to stare at me.

"What?" I asked.

Pedersen clasped his hands behind his dark blond head and leaned back in his chair. "I've thought of a question, the answer to which might be of extreme interest."

"Oh?"

"Have any baggage handlers left their jobs recently? Say, at the end of last week?"

"You're asking me?" I drew a red circle around a possible error in the listing I was studying, already dotted with so many red circles it looked as if it had caught a loathesome disease.

"Perhaps I could telephone Budjetair," Pedersen mused.

I closed my eyes to keep from groaning.

"You can call anybody you damn please," I said. "I've got to get this stuff caught up by Friday."

"Working your poor skull to the bone," Pedersen sighed, reaching for the telephone.

"A skull is a bone, lunkhead." I circled what might be another error. Numbers, numbers. Six days away had been too long: what the hell did they all mean? Did I even have the right printout? I glanced at the top of the page: Jamison. I was the only Jamison around, so I went back to studying the numbers.

"Oh, he won't be in all day?" Pedersen said into the telephone. "Maybe you could help me." The face of the kid with the Mylar balloons floated through my mind, as if attached to a string and filled with helium. Twelve hundred miles, count 'em, just like my car had. I was damn lucky the weather had held, Karen was right about that, or I might have been holed up in a motel in Grand Forks or Devil's Lake, with the Fairmont nothing but the core of a drift on the highway. And even that would be lucky, not to be in the car.

Pedersen dialed again. He hadn't talked very long. I shrugged the thought away and tried to focus on the work in front of me. What I thought was: I had a snow survival kit in the car, *which Karen had put together,* and a brain in my head. The survival kit was a three-pound coffee can with a fat candle and waterproof matches; dry soup, cocoa, and coffee to mix with snow water boiled in the can set over the candle; a couple of plastic trash bags for emergency boots or blankets; and a red flag for the car's antenna. *And Karen knew damn well* I had a sleeping bag in the back seat, and sand and a snow shovel in the trunk, dry socks and mittens and scarf and hat, the whole works, even an old pair of jeans, except that Joey had found the candy bars and eaten a hole in the wrapper of each one and I'd never gotten around to buying any more. *Well, and who needed them?* The brain was standard issue, good enough to go on with. I'd exercised it by thinking of words to fit around the letters of the license plates ahead of me. Some tough combinations, too: QDP, quadruple. DZS, adzes. UFZ, sulfathiazole. Karen hadn't had one word of sympathy for that endless drive. . . .

"Thank you very much," Pedersen said. He hung up and grazed at me from under his pale lashes with a satisfied smirk. "It's Mr. Basil Devitt's day for racquetball, as I might have guessed, but his secretary was able to direct me to the baggage handling pool that serves the small independent airlines. And they" – the smirk widened into a wolfish grin – "told me that Mr. Leonard Fink, familiarly known as Lenny, left their employ only last Friday."

I looked at the wall beyond my desk. Karen's face, four years younger than it was at home, smiled back at me. "How long had he planned to retire?"

Pedersen's grin faded. "I didn't ask. However, I have a home address and a telephone number, and I plan to interview Mr. Fink at my earliest convenience."

"Coincidence," I said. I swirled the sludge in the bottom of my plastic cup and decided not to drink it.

"Jamison, this is January of 1983. Nobody, *nobody,* gives up a secure, well-paying job in January of 1983." Pedersen leaned forward for emphasis. "Want to toss for coffee?"

I dug a quarter out of my pocket and flipped it. "Tails," I called.

Heads it was. If Pedersen ever had to buy coffee for me I would probably have a heart attack on the spot and not be around to enjoy drinking the free foul brew. I used to think it was some kind of trick he did, but it's been going on for years, so it's got to be luck. Not that I can grudge it: Pedersen hit the top salary for his grade quite a while ago, and the raises within grades don't nearly keep up with inflation. With six kids – well.

I got up and wandered out to the machine, in front of which I was invited once more to toss for treat, pled prior disadvantage, and bought two more cups of kidney rot.

When I got back to the cubicle I share with Pedersen, he was on the phone again, so I just replaced the empty cup on the far right corner of his desk with a full one and got back to work myself.

Midafternoon, the phone rang. Pedersen scooped it up eagerly and made a little moue of disappointment. "For you," he said, holding the receiver at arm's length, and, with the other hand, typing into the computer terminal we share.

"J.J."

"Karen? What's up?" She sounded strained.

"J.J. Do you remember Aunt Agatha?"

I drew another red circle. "Your Aunt Agatha?" Oh, lord, some other of Karen's passel of relatives I'd forgotten. At least it couldn't be anyone too vital, anyone she'd talked about a lot.

"Jane's mother," she said hurriedly. "J.J., there's a problem with Aunt Agatha I've got to see about, OK?"

"I guess so." Damn, another mistake. I might as well start all over from the beginning; it would save time. Pedersen's chair squeaked and I glanced over to see him making monster claws at the telephone in my hand. *Gimme*, he mouthed.

"My Aunt Agatha," Karen repeated. "Jane's mother. I don't know how long it will take, but hope for me there's no funeral to go to, OK? Oh!" she babbled. "Good-bye."

"OK," I said, remembering the irritated frenzy of shopping for suitable clothes when her grandmother died, a few years ago, but she had already hung up. Pedersen snatched the phone from my hand and dialed, put the receiver down on the terminal, punched in his name and password, and sighed happily. I went back to drawing red circles, and only when I came up for air at the end of a page did it dawn on me that Karen had called me J.J.

Only two people in my life don't call me J.J. One is Pedersen, who calls everyone including his wife by some version of their surname, and the other is Karen, who has always called me Joe, although even my mother uses the initials. Was she trying to tell me something?

If so, the message hadn't come through. I thought about calling her back, but

Pedersen put his hand on the phone, still cradled on the terminal, and growled, so I shook my head and applied myself to my art work. By four-thirty, when the general stir around me roused me again, I'd forgotten all about the call. I went out to the parking lot with a flash of my badge, praying that the Ford would start.

For once, it started like a charm. I headed home with the radio tuned to KSJN. *All Things Considered* was well underway when I pulled into my driveway and stared, perplexed, at my dark house.

I looked for a note when I got in, but there was nothing on the woodgrain Formica table but a peeling swipe of oatmeal where Joey had sat in a big chair for breakfast. Problem with writing wives. They don't get much housework done.

I tossed my coat onto the back of a chair and levered my boots off. Sock-footed, I crossed the cold vinyl tile to the shag rug of the family room and looked for a note on the bulletin board. Nothing.

Not like Karen not to leave a note. Unless, of course, she was only next door? I used the kitchen phone to try calling Mrs. Eskew: the phone rang and rang. I counted to thirty in case I'd summoned her arthritic old joints from a hot bath, and gave up. Celia Dixon, on the other side, had just arrived home herself.

"Honestly, J.J. She probably just ran out to pick up something for dinner – she'll be home soon." Celia laughed as she hung up.

I couldn't picture Karen shoving Joey in the stroller through the snowy sidewalks, half a mile to the nearest place she could get anything for dinner. Puzzled, I explored the kitchen. Lunch dishes in the sink, rinsed and ready for the dishwasher. A package of pork chops in the refrigerator, plenty of frozen vegetables in the top. Rice, noodles, potatoes – she wouldn't have had to go out. And even if she had, wouldn't she have waited until I got home with the car?

I trotted into the bedroom for my slippers, flipped on the overhead light, and stopped dead.

Karen's dresser drawers were standing open. All seven years of our married life, Karen had nagged me to close drawers, shut cupboards, turn off lights, water, the oven, you name it. The first inkling of real fear touched me.

Jeans, shirts, underwear missing. In Joey's room, I couldn't be as sure. But the drawers were standing open there, too, and some of the overalls and shirts I remembered weren't in the drawers. I dug through his smelly laundry to be sure. Where would Karen have taken Joey, without telling me? To *visit* her aunt?

Address book. I went through the whole thing, page by page. No Agatha. The only Jane was someone I knew, Karen's old college roommate, no relation.

"She'll call," I said aloud, instantly sorry I had spoken. The words almost echoed.

I went back to the family room and sprawled on the couch with the network news on, trying to lose my uneasiness in other people's troubles. Some very bad weather had hit most of the country but our own small patch: floods in the south, rain in California, heavy snow in the east. So far, our own winter had been mild beyond belief. I decided to take that as an omen: what could go wrong in a winter like this one? Feet propped on the coffee table, I even watched the ads.

At six, I tried Mrs. Eskew again. No answer.

As I turned back toward the television I saw the paperback on the coffee table for the first time. *Read, that's it, J.J.* A good mystery to keep your mind from going in circles. I picked up the book, one Karen had been reading before I left for balloon-ridden Bottineau.

Nemesis, by Agatha Christie. A Miss Jane Marple mystery.

Aunt Agatha. Jane's mother.

Hope for me there's no funeral to go to.

I felt as if my belly had drained onto the floor. "God damn it, Karen, why couldn't you just come right out and tell me what was wrong?" I shouted into the empty house.

The answer came as fast as the question: because someone was with her. Someone threatening her. Someone who wouldn't let her say what was wrong. I dropped the book and lunged for the kitchen phone.

The calm, efficient voice at the other end of the line decided that my call wasn't really a 911 emergency and suggested that I call the precinct station direct. She gave me the number. I poked at the buttons. The voice in the precinct station was dry and bored, but promised to send someone out to talk to me right away.

I should have saved my breath. The detective who came, not what I'd call right away but not all that much later, took notes on everything I had to say but was not convinced that anything was really wrong.

"I'm telling you," I repeated, sure that if I could just explain my point clearly enough, the man would be as alarmed as I was. "She called me J.J. She *never* calls me J.J. She pointed out this book. It's a *murder* mystery, for God's sake," I pleaded, punching the girl on the cover in the nose. "Can't you understand? She said to hope there wasn't a funeral."

"I still don't see that you should worry, Mr. Jamison," the detective said gently. "She could have gone out shopping, like your neighbor said. She might have met a friend and time got away from her, you know how it does. She could walk in that door any minute."

I shook my head. "Not Karen. She'd have left me a note, she'd have told me when she called. Somebody had to be with her, somebody who wouldn't let her talk, or she wouldn't have gone through his business with the name and the book."

The detective, a large, lined man with heavy eyebrows, sighed. "You think that, sure. What's to say she's not playing a joke? To see how you react?"

"Listen, you hairy bastard. My wife's been kidnapped!"

He didn't flinch, not even when I jumped out of my chair and started pacing. "Look, she's been gone, what? Three hours at the outside. She's got the kid with her. She went out to see a friend, take it from me, or she went shopping. Maybe got hung up in traffic."

"No car," I objected.

"The friend's car. Nothing's missing, right?"

"Just some clothes."

"Just some clothes." He wrote that down. "You could have mentioned that sooner, it makes a little difference. Any sign of a struggle?"

I looked at the room: all exactly as usual, looking a little shabby, suddenly. "No."

"So, odds are, she's gone of her own free will and she'll be back when she feels like it. Happens all the time, Mr. Jamison. I wouldn't get all upset, if I were you."

I stared at him, at the heavy shadow of his chin, at the short black hairs on his nose that looked as if he had to shave that, too, at times. "You think she just walked out?"

The guy looked at me, measuring the distance between us. I called him a few names that made as much impression as pebbles falling into a bog. He sighed again, stood up, and flipped his notebook shut. "Look," he said. "I know you're frustrated and I know you're upset. But I really think you're being a little premature, understand? You get any threats, any demands for ransom, anything like that, you let me know right away. You've got my name, you've got my phone number, leave a message anytime day or night and I'll get it. And let me know when you hear from your wife."

If I hear from my wife, I thought, slamming the door behind him. *If* I hear from my wife.

I leaned my forehead against the cool wood of the front door until I heard a car door shut outside, the grind of a starter motor. Odds are, she's gone of her own free will. The engine caught, the sound faded away.

I dragged myself back to the family room and slumped on the couch, where I'd sat the night before as Karen tried to get me to give up CATCH. I'd barely said I'd think about it.

Maybe it had been too much. Maybe the six days I'd been gone, the lost chance to spend a few days in the Florida sun, had been the straw that broke the camel's back.

Or maybe while I'd been gallivanting over the prairies in search of silver balloons, Karen had done some gallivanting of her own and found somebody who liked to stay home nights with his feet up on the coffee table, watching whatever came on TV, a guy right there with a hand to run down the groove of her back and a shoulder to snuggle against whenever she wanted. . . .

The first I'd ever had such a doubt. It stung.

Karen didn't call. She didn't come home. I spent the night in Joey's new big bed and got up before five, smelling of baby powder.

Chapter Five

I paced and puttered for an hour, and managed only to tie my stomach in knots. Might as well go to work, I decided: if Karen . . . changed her mind . . . that was where she'd expect to find me, wasn't it? And if . . . somebody else . . . wanted to call me, that's where he'd call, right? To find a working man on a Thursday morning? One thing sure. If I didn't stop cracking my knuckles pretty soon, my fingers were likely to pop right off.

Just to cover all bases, I wrote a note to Karen asking her please, please to call me the instant she got home. As I put it on the kitchen table I noticed the smear of dried oatmeal again and started to wipe it up. I couldn't do it. Instead, I tossed the sponge back into the sink, stepped ten years back in time, and drew along the bottom of the note the row of hearts I'd have been too shy to add as a sophomore in college.

The night man was still at the guard desk when I walked into the plant. He had to check my name against a list of employees despite my badge: what I got for shaving off my mustache after the picture was taken. I told the guard my birth date and Social Security number. He didn't even grin as he nodded me through. The company was locking the barn door good and tight while Aunt Yuk cantered through unknown fields of daisies. Typical.

From the guard desk a long hall, bleak at this time of morning with only every third light on, leads back through the building, past the cafeteria to the stairwell. The stairs echoed as I climbed, and the light from the wide windows at the landing was the faint mauve of a winter dawn.

Strange to see Pedersen's desk without a scrap of paper on it, pencils in a neat row, the chair pushed in, all the stained Styrofoam cups whisked away by the cleaning crew. My own desk was its usual mess. I sat down, took the picture of Karen off the wall and tucked it into my center desk drawer, and put my head in my hands.

It was still there when Pedersen came in and mock-staggered backward out the door. "Jamison!" he exclaimed. "Has the Last Trumpet sounded?" He tiptoed into the cubicle, yanked his chair away from his desk, and plunked into it.

I took a shallow breath and held it a

moment. Behind me, Pedersen clunked and rustled, getting papers out of his desk drawers. "Eh?" he prompted.

"Could be." I saw a couple of damp spots wrinkling the listing in front of me and dabbed at them with my sleeve, but they were old, sunk too far into the paper to wipe up, and all I accomplished was pink stain on my shirt sleeve where one of my red circles had run. I rubbed my fingers over my cheeks as if trying to wake myself up and yawned.

"Such industry," Pedersen commented as he banged a few sheets of paper into a neat stack. "Do you plan to use the terminal, or may I have it?"

"You can use it."

"Codes are getting tougher and tougher to break, these days," Pedersen observed. "Even I frequently have difficulty."

I smiled in spite of myself. Whatever Pedersen was having difficulty with, it wasn't part of his job, so I refrained from asking. Once before he'd surprised me with a lot of information he shouldn't have had, all obtained courtesy of his fingers flying over a keyboard. An embarrassment, really, but useful at the time. That's not to say that I didn't wonder what had brought him in early.

He punched buttons on the telephone and

set the receiver down in the terminal's cradle. "Leonard Fink, your secrets shall be opened unto me," he intoned. "Only I can't find your bank account. Or whether you've got a Visa card."

"Shut up, Lars," I said. "You want the whole world to know what you're doing? You could get yourself –"

"Into a lot of trouble," he chimed in. "Except that you and I are the only ones here. Do you or do you not wish to discover where and with whom Aunt Yuk has absconded?"

"I'd settle for Karen."

Pedersen's forefinger, hovering over the transmit button, instead punched *off*. "Karen is missing?"

I nodded. "She called me yesterday afternoon, remember? Only I was too stupid to catch on that something was wrong, even when she called me 'J.J.' instead of 'Joe.' She never called me J.J. in her life, you know that."

Pedersen nodded wisely.

"And then she gave me this funny story about her Aunt Agatha and her cousin, Jane. She's got a million relatives and I'm always losing track of them, so I didn't think too much about not recognizing the names, but when I got home I found this Agatha Christie novel on the coffee table, one with

Jane Marple in it. Called *Nemesis.*" I shivered slightly. "And she said for me to hope that there isn't a funeral, and there's no Agatha in her address book."

"She hoped to convey a message."

"Sure, but I don't know what it was. She took some clothes and Joey, and she left all the drawers standing open, she *never* leaves drawers hanging out, and she didn't come home –"

Pedersen's quicker than some detectives I know. "Kidnapped. Someone with her, so that she could not speak freely. And to do with Aunt Yuk, without a doubt. Have you contacted the police?"

I sighed. "Yeah, but they don't take it very seriously. Jerk told me she'd probably just run off."

"Perhaps as well," Pedersen mused. "I'm not sure what we should say to them about the pattern discriminator. How much have you told them?"

"About Aunt Yuk? Nothing. The connection didn't occur to me, to tell the truth."

Pedersen's eyebrows shot up. "But the use of *aunt* in her code is surely significant?"

"It could be. I don't know. She does know the discriminator is missing." I dug the heels of my hands into my burning eyes and yawned again. "I left a note for her to call me, if she comes home."

Pedersen put a hand on my knee, squeezed briefly, and turned back to the terminal. "Now we really do have to find this Leonard Fink and ask him some questions. He is our only . . . lead, is it? But his telephone is unresponsive, last night and again this morning."

"Maybe he decided not to quit, after all."

"Sensible, but unlikely. He can hardly work every hour of the day." Pedersen shook his head testily, and I slumped back onto my desk. The brief cheer I'd felt at the prospect of help evaporated. What the hell did I think a crazy engineer with a genius for poking his long nose into other people's computers could do to find my wife?

The terminal chattered for a moment.

I heard the rip of paper from the printer, a sigh, and then Pedersen racketed out of the cubicle. Someone came up the stairs and a chair clanked nearby. A few minutes later, other feet climbed the stairs. A greeting was spoken. The day was about to get underway. I stared at the yellowed tag of cellophane tape that had held Karen's picture on my wall for the last couple of years, thinking. Should I read that book? Was there a clue in the plot? Or was Karen only trying to say, things are not as they seem, check them out?

Pedersen returned and set a plate with two corn muffins and two pats of butter on them down on my desk, along with a Styrofoam container of coffee with a lid. "You've probably neglected your morning nutriments," he said. "Eat."

"Where'd you get this?"

"In the cafeteria, of course. Not everyone works first shift." He pulled some paper out of his pocket, the printout he'd torn off as he left, and stared at it gloomily. Touched, I buttered one muffin – they were even hot – and choked it down.

"One night imagine that this Leonard Fink has endeavored to elude every computer in the nation," Pedersen complained. "I don't think I have entered senility just yet. But what does the man do? He must drive, he must buy things."

"Just a taxpayer like the rest of us," I agreed through the second muffin. Pedersen had been right: I was hungry, and my stomach knew it even if my brain wasn't bright enough to catch on.

"Taxpayer," Pedersen breathed.

Me and my big mouth. "Watch it, Lars," I warned, but he was already probing the keyboard, mouth pursed.

The phone rang three minutes after Pedersen gave up on Lenny Fink. He was staring into space, too engrossed in thought to hear anything so mundane as a telephone. I picked it up and said, "Two-oh-three-nine, Jamison."

"Mr. Jamison, is your wife named Karen?" someone whispered.

"Yes." I felt again as if the contents of my torso had melted and run out.

"Then listen carefully," the whisperer said. In the background, I could hear a child crying. "You must drop your investigation immediately. If, after ten days, it has not continued, your wife and son will be returned to you unharmed."

"Who –" But the man had hung up. "Oh, dear God," I groaned.

Pedersen slowly brought his gaze down and focused on me.

"He wants us to stop the investigation," I said, pulling the man's words out of the crying that had distracted me. "If we hold off for ten days, Karen and Joey can come home."

"Ten days. Plenty of time to take the pattern discriminator apart and determine how it works," Pedersen observed. "I think we must go and speak to R. Quentin at once, don't you?"

At first I thought my boss would pee his pants. I knew the feeling well. That lasted about ten seconds, and then I thought he was going to launch himself across his desk and throttle me.

"Who the hell did you tell about this, J.J.?" he demanded. His voice was low and gritty: I'd have been happier if he'd yelled. "Don't you know what *confidential* means? Jeez, if this is out –"

"I didn't tell anyone."

"You must have! How else would they know to take your wife?"

I looked to Pedersen for a cue and got none. "I don't have any idea how it got out, Bob," I said, as placating as I could be.

R. Quentin wasn't placated. "How much did you tell the cops?"

"About Aunt Yuk? Nothing. I didn't make the connection until this morning."

R. Quentin locked his fingers in what was left of his hair and tugged. He took a deep breath between his teeth. "I don't understand this at all! Not at all! What am I going to do now?"

Pedersen cleared his throat. "I suggest we do nothing."

"Now, wait a minute," I shouted. "We're talking about my wife and son! This is just what it will take to get the cops serious about finding them, can't you see that? Do you think I give a damn about some machine when my family's in danger?"

"Jamison –" Pedersen said.

"You can build another pattern recognizer, damn it. I can't build another wife. I can't build another son."

R. Quentin took three deep breaths that whistled in his nose. "Look, J.J. I appreciate your concern," he began.

Hell you do, I thought.

"But you must realize that there's another interest involved here, maybe even a national interest. We *must* recover Aunt Yuk. If you prefer not to work on the investigation yourself, I can understand that, but I think it only fair to warn you that your refusal will go on your personnel records, and when it comes time for your annual review –"

"Stuff your annual review."

Pedersen inserted a hand and a smile into the argument. "Excuse me," he said. "Why can't Jamison just go to the police and tell them he's had a call asking for ransom?"

R. Quentin sat back in his chair and sucked at his lower lip for several seconds. "Keep us out of it entirely, you mean?"

"Exactly."

"They're going to want to know why he was contacted at work and not at home."

"I'm sure it can't be that unusual," Pedersen soothed.

"How would the kidnapper get his number? Here, I mean?"

"Ask his wife," Pedersen said. "How else? Unless, of course, it's someone so close he wouldn't need to do so."

"Here?" I asked.

R. Quentin frowned. "He could be right, I guess," he allowed. "The person who intercepted the shipment had to know where it was going, and when. So I guess it's not so surprising that he'd know where to phone you."

Not from the next cubicle. A whisper might carry that far. But from the pay phone in the lobby . . . the little structure of hope I had built on the idea that Karen was necessary to give out the phone number crumpled.

"What I want to know," R. Quentin continued, rotating his chair slowly back and forth, "is, how did they know you were the one to phone?"

"My wife –"

"Yes, of course, but that only leads back to my other question. How did they know *your* wife and son were the ones to take?"

"Perhaps they chose Karen and Joey because two are easier to manage than seven," Pedersen suggested, deliberately obtuse.

R. Quentin blew a sigh through his nose. "Look, you two. I'm not going to have you running another circus here. I asked you to help because I thought that with your various areas of expertise, legal and illegal" – here he looked at Pedersen, not at me – "you might be able to shake something loose. Now it looks like whoever's behind this shook you loose. So now quit. We'll leave it all to ARA, maybe get the guy to come here if he has to. I'm sure that when Jim Kochel gets back, he'll approve." He shifted in his chair to underscore his knowledge of his own boss, leaned on his desk, and smiled at me. "In the meantime, J.J., I invite you to use my phone to call the police and tell them about this demand for ransom."

"I can hardly stand the honor."

He pushed the phone toward me, not smiling. "Call."

"What do I tell them?"

"Just that you've heard from the kidnapper, your wife and son are being held, and you will be contacted with details for a ransom drop later."

I turned that over for a minute. "I don't like it."

"You don't have to like it. You just have to do it."

It seemed safe enough. At least it would get the cops more interested in finding Karen, and if they fell over the Aunt Yuk business in the process, the company could probably persuade them to keep quiet. *R. Quentin's problem,* I thought as I hunted through my wallet for the hairy detective's card. I dialed 9 and waited for the outside dial tone. "This better work," I said.

"It's a hard job market," my boss remarked.

He had probably checked the Sunday papers for an escape route, while I was on my innocent way back from Bottineau via Grand Forks. I dialed. Beside me, Pedersen crossed his legs the other way over. The detective wasn't in, and I left a message.

"That's all?" asked the voice taking the message. "Just, you'll be contacted later? No dollar amount?"

"That's right."

"Thanks. We'll be in touch."

I put the phone down and stared at R. Quentin, who wouldn't meet my eyes. "That will do, for now," he said. "But remember, my main question hasn't been answered yet. Not satisfactorily. Not at all, in fact."

Pedersen jumped out of his seat, and I

followed him out of R. Quentin's office, which, I reflected, was, except for having a window, almost a ringer for the one Budjetair had provided for its president. As I shut the door, I heard the low grind of the telephone dial.

"Do you recall that Burns was divorced last year?" Pedersen asked quietly, when we were some way down the hall.

"Sort of."

"His wife got tired of his emotional involvement with the company and took a lover, whom she found she preferred. She told him precisely why. You might remember that, in dealing with him."

"Thanks. I'll keep it in mind."

"Vindictive woman," Pedersen commented. He turned left into our cubicle, and I followed him in and collapsed into my chair. Pedersen rolled his own chair straight to the terminal and began to fiddle with it. I wished he'd stop.

The day was long and hard, but driving home was longer and harder. I felt a flurry of hope as I drove up to the garage: a light was on in the kitchen, another in the living room. I let myself in with my heart knocking on all four cylinders, calling, "Karen? Joey?"

No answer. My note was still on the

kitchen table, just as I had left it. But my heart didn't start to slow until I had searched the entire house, and found the rest of it also precisely as I had left it that morning. I must have left the lights on myself. There was another on in Joey's room and one in our bedroom, and the bathtub tap was dripping.

I'd been home long enough to rinse out the coffeepot and set it up again when the doorbell rang. Another speed-up for the old cardiovascular system, but it wasn't Karen locked out, just the same hairy detective who'd come the night before, as big as ever, and no smiles.

"So you heard from somebody," he greeted me.

I nodded. "Come in."

The invitation was superfluous, issued as he was closing the door with his ass, but he said, "Thanks."

"Come on into the kitchen. I'm making coffee," I said. He clumped after me and balanced his butt on one of our kitchen chairs, which had never looked particularly fragile before. "You want to hear about this telephone call."

"That was the general idea."

"Well, this guy called me at work and said he had my wife and she wasn't hurt. I could hear a kid crying. It could have been Joey, it sounded like him." The notebook was out and the guy was writing in it, what looked like Speedwriting: *U kn gt a gd jb & mor pa.* With R. Quentin in the mood he was in, maybe I should take the course myself. "He said he'd call back, let me know about a ransom."

"That's all?"

"That's all."

"He didn't tell you, get so much together by such-and-such time?"

"No."

"Hmm." It wasn't going over. "He said I, not we?"

"I think so." What in hell had I told the guy at the precinct station? I couldn't remember, and ten to one they had it on tape. The percolator cut off and I poured coffee. "Anything in it?"

"Black, thanks." He watched while I doctored my own with the last of the milk. "What kind of voice did this guy have?"

"Dunno. He whispered."

"Any particular accent? Foreign, east coast, southern?"

I shrugged. *Mdwst,* the detective wrote.

"What should I do?"

He looked around the kitchen, picked a little at the flaking oatmeal on the table. I wanted to belt him one. Why I should attach such importance to that little bit of junk, I still don't know. "Sit tight," he advised. "Let me know right away if the guy calls again."

I sat down behind my coffee. The detective took a sip of his. "Frankly, Mr. Jamison, I got to wonder about this. Last night you tell me your wife and kid aren't here, she's made a funny phone call, you don't know where she went. I tell you if anybody contacts you, let me know. Presto, the next morning somebody calls you at work, no demands, no arrangements, just, I'll let you know. You know what that could look like?"

"I didn't make it up," I said, maybe too quickly.

"Sure, sure." The notebook was open again, the pages flipping. "Listen to this. Statement from Mrs. LeFleur from across the street. You know her?"

"Candy LeFleur, sure."

"She got anything against you? You got anything against her?"

Nothing but the way she spelled her last name. I shook my head.

"Fine. Here's what she's got to say. She was sitting on her couch, knitting and looking out her front window yesterday afternoon around three or three-thirty, and she saw your wife coming out your front door with a man. Mrs. LeFleur doesn't know the man. Tall, that's all she can tell me, and white. The guy is carrying your kid, and your wife goes around to the garage and opens the door and a minute later she comes out with the kid's car seat. She goes down the driveway and unlocks a car standing at the curb. Red late-model two-door sedan. The guy is still holding your kid, and your kid is laughing and he pulls the guy's nose, and the guy looks like he's laughing, too. Your wife crawls into the car and puts the car seat in and gets into the driver's seat. Then the guy puts your kid in the car seat, which is on the left side in the back which is where your wife has once told Mrs. LeFleur it's safest. Your wife scoots across the seat and the guy gets in and slams the door and the three of them drive away happy as clams, she says. Oh, yeah, and your wife also has a suitcase which she tosses into the trunk before she fixes the kid's car seat. Now, Mr. Jamison, does that sound like your typical kidnapping?"

"It had to be. Karen wouldn't –"

"Nobody struggling? People laughing?"

I couldn't find anything to say.

"I'll tell you, Mr. Jamison. In all my experience, I never heard of a kidnapper giving his victim time to pack." He eyed me a moment. "You and your wife had any arguments lately? Like, what about what Mrs. LeFleur says here, you were gone six days on vacation by yourself and your wife had to borrow a neighbor's car to get around in?"

"She borrowed Candy's car?" Somehow, I couldn't see Karen slushing through the streets in a lime-green Corvette.

"No, it says here, from Mrs. Eskew. I haven't talked to the lady yet, she hasn't been home. But I can't say I've got anything yet that makes me real worried, Mr. Jamison. So, until I get a little hard evidence to work on, I'm just going to sit tight, and that's what I recommend you do, too."

It was even a lot of fun when I could go along. . . . Maybe Karen wanted some adventure, someone in her life a little more... swashbuckling. But it's hard for a man to swash any bucklers when he wears a plastic nerd pouch in his shirt pocket five days a week.... "I don't believe it," I said weakly. "I just don't believe it."

"Maybe your wife met a tall, dark, and handsome." *Like Angela Burns did.* "Happens to everybody, just like I say. So, you sit tight and see what happens." The jackass got up and walked through my house and let himself out. I walked through the house after him and turned the deadbolt and put the chain up and kicked the door good and hard.

My coffee was cold. The detective hadn't drunk more than that one sip. I picked up the cup he had used and threw it at the back door, which was dumb because then I had to wipe a lot of coffee off the floor, the four walls, and even the ceiling, and get rid of a mess of broken crockery.

Well, it passed the evening. I found the surgical tape in the linen closet and taped up the one small cut I'd given myself, remembered to put the tape back, and even remembered to close the closet door.

Chapter Six

I was exhausted when I finally crawled into bed, my own this time, but I didn't sleep. When I closed my eyes I saw splashes of coffee on the glossy white background of the kitchen cabinets; when I opened them the dark ceiling seemed to be lowering on me. Either way, I was thinking about other kidnappings I'd read about: a banker's wife chained to a tree in the woods, a girl locked into a storage shed for days on end, a kid left in the trunk of a car just like mine, in which I'd brought a dozen eggs home from the supermarket last winter and opened the carton in the house to find the eggs already frozen, the shells cracked and the whites reproaching me.

The weather the past few days had been mild, balmy for January; people had been joking about lazing on the beach. But the temperature had taken a big drop when the sun went down: the thermometer outside the kitchen window had read four above zero just before I went to bed. An adult with her wits about her might find some way to survive in that cold, but a thirty-pound kid nowhere near three feet tall, who couldn't even keep his pants dry? I kept falling into half-dreams: Karen pounding on the door, which brought me awake already half out of bed and calling out that I was coming, don't go away; Joey frozen on the doorstep when I opened the door to take in the newspaper, which woke me with my own moan.

When I had finally slept, and wakened again, it was no better. Mindful of Pedersen's corn muffins, and encouraged by a stomach that had had no dinner for the second night in a row, I threw down some dry shredded wheat and a hunk of liverwurst for breakfast, but the contrast of the silent house with the usual morning bustle drove me to work early again. I left the note I'd written the day before on the kitchen table, more as a good luck charm than because I had any hope that Karen would come home to read it. The roads were dark. Not even enough cars to play the license plate game to keep my mind occupied.

Early as I was, Pedersen was there before me. He cocked his head at me without speaking.

"No news."

He drew a deep breath that whistled faintly in his nose. "Have you had breakfast?"

"Today, yes." He hunched his fingers over the keyboard of the computer terminal. "Still after Lenny Fink?"

"Alas."

I had been sitting at my desk making red circles for quite a while when I heard R. Quentin Burns asking for Bill Chapin in the cubicle next door. Odd, I thought. I hadn't seen Bill since I got back, and here I had been supposed to be investigating how he'd come to misplace our most valuable piece of equipment. "Let me know when he comes in," R. Quentin said, out in the hall. A moment later he was standing at our door. "Good news," he said cheerfully. "We found Aunt Yuk."

"Found her! Where?"

"This ARA guy is apparently as efficient as his reputation says he is. He just walked into Los Angeles International airport, hunted through some logical places, and came up with our prodigal lady."

"Excellent," Pedersen said, without perceptible enthusiasm.

"One of the L.A. people is bringing her east for our hardware gang to check out. And not on Budjetair."

"You ought to tell Basil Devitt," I said. "Maybe he'd go dance on a runway and get run down."

"I should tell him she's been found, at least," Burns said. "You didn't make any threats, did you, Lars?"

"No."

"Good. I'd hate to look like the damn fool I feel." R. Quentin trod jauntily away. Feeling a damn fool was apparently good for him.

Pedersen remained faced away from his desk and pulled at his chin, a habit of his that may account for its length. "You know, it might almost look as if the discriminator had simply been misplaced," he said.

"Might?"

"Except that your wife is still missing."

I propped my head in my hands and stared down at my elbows. "I can't help that." The most reasonable explanation of all of it popped into my head. Aunt Yuk *had* simply been misplaced. Karen had cooked up that call with this guy, whoever he was.... I'd told her about the investigation, and she wanted me out of it. But who was the guy? And Karen? Karen, who had always been open and honest with me before... who had always *seemed* to be open and honest.... "I'm being poisoned," I muttered, and pulled together some corrected programs to check on the big computers in the room down the hall. *If she just wanted to teach me a lesson,* I thought, *she didn't have to go this far.*

I was watching the little gray characters wink on the screen when Burns found me, half an hour later. "Leave that, J.J.," he said. "I've got another job for you. Bill Chapin hasn't come in for a couple of days. Could you run out to his place and roust him out?"

"Can't you phone him?"

"I tried. He doesn't answer." My boss looked at his fingernails. "I gave him Tuesday off because he was upset, but he wasn't in Wednesday or yesterday, either, and I'm getting worried. He could have taken this business too much to heart."

"Bill?"

"Go out and check, anyway, will you? That stuff can wait. Lisa has the address."

"I want Lars with me," I said, with a sudden qualm. What if I found Karen and Joey with Bill Chapin? Now that he had enough plumbing to go around? She'd known right away who he was. . . .

"Lars has a lot of work to do."

"I'm not going by myself."

"Have it your way." He shrugged.

It didn't seem all that urgent, so I finished loading my program to see if it would run. To my considerable surprise, it started off right away. I got another engineer, Wilmot, to babysit it and went to collect Lars Pedersen.

We took my Ford, since my nerves weren't up to Pedersen's driving. The address Lisa had given me was for a new building, built overlooking the Mississippi in what in my youth had been one of the more run-down areas of town. I found a spot in the guest parking area and ran the nose of the Fairmont as far into the crestfallen snowbank at the end of the slot as it would go.

"Think he's skipped town?" I asked, as Pedersen and I skirted the slushy puddles of the parking lot.

"I've been puzzling over that." Pedersen lent credence to his words with a tight frown. "If he had an arrangement with someone – but now that Aunt Yuk has been found, it doesn't look that way . . . but it could have been made not to look that way. . . ." He looked up at the sleek brown brick side of the building and shook his head. "That doesn't make sense. Because if it was meant to look as if she was only misplaced, what had Chapin to fear? And if he wasn't part of the plan, then what had he to fear? Less, surely. So I think he has not fled," he concluded. "Further, if he was part of the plan and it had been made to look as if nothing much happened, surely he would have been well paid and it would be to his advantage to stay, ready to earn more money in similar ways." He had opened the outer glass door of the building and now examined the row of door-bells above the brass mailboxes in the outer lobby. "And, most of all, why kidnap your wife?"

Maybe I had an answer to that, but I didn't want to make it real by saying it.

"Ah, here he is." Pedersen pressed firmly on the oval black button under the card that said *William C. Chapin III,* and we waited. After a few minutes, he pressed it again.

A woman pushed through the doors from the parking lot with two armloads of groceries. She gave us a mistrustful glance, apparently decided that two decently dressed men posed no immediate threat, and began to juggle her bags and her purse. "May I assist you?" Pedersen asked. He turned up the wattage of his blue eyes. A little more of his lilting accent came into his words. "Perhaps, hold the groceries?"

"Oh. Yeah, sure, thanks." Pedersen stood holding the bags while the woman rummaged for her key and applied it to the inner lock. I held the door for her and Pedersen handed over the bags. She smiled and disappeared into the open elevator opposite the door.

As the elevator doors slid shut, Pedersen stepped into the inner vestibule. "Since Chapin hasn't answered his bell, it may be out of order," he said. "Let's go knock. We can use the stairs, it's only the third floor."

But Chapin didn't answer our knock, although the rap of Pedersen's knuckles sounded authoritative enough. Pedersen reached into his inside coat pocket for his wallet.

I felt a small click of recognition. Something I'd met before. "Hold on, Lars."

I stopped his hand before he could slide his Visa card into the crack of the door. "That's breaking and entering. And I think we'd be better off with a witness for this."

"Good thought," he conceded. "I wonder where the building superintendent would be at this hour?"

We went back down to the outer lobby and looked for a bell for the super. "Shut that door," Pedersen said. "We want to look perfectly innocent, as you so wisely pointed out." I wondered if he already knew what had happened to Chapin. As I let the inner door fall shut he punched the bell. "We say only that he has not come to work for several days and we wish to check that he is all right," he reminded me, as if I hadn't told him that myself. "It's possible we are making fools of ourselves. Ah."

A little, hollow-templed old guy in a plaid shirt and bib overalls had come through a door opposite the stairs in the inner vestibule. He opened the glass door a crack, as if he had it on a chain. "What you guys want?"

I let Pedersen do the talking, again. He was by far the more presentable of us: I'd noticed circles under my eyes while I was shaving that morning, and besides, I couldn't keep my mind off Karen and Joey.

"Two days?" the super said doubtfully.

"Three. And he's urgently needed at work," Pedersen was saying. "He hasn't called in. Very unlike him."

"Sick, you think?"

"I really don't know. But it's possible. That's why we came over to check on him."

"Mmm." The super scratched his chin and opened the door wide enough for us to step through. "Can't hurt to check, I s'pose," he decided. "Hate to think of him maybe laying there sick and no help." He went back into his lair for a moment and returned with a ring of keys. "You guys work with him, you said?" he confirmed, pressing the elevator call button.

"Yes." That was Pedersen. "Our boss

asked us to come by and see why he hasn't shown up."

"Coulda called," the superintendent said, stepping into the elevator. I could hear relief in his voice: boss was evidently a word he understood.

He slipped through the brass doors as they opened and trudged down the hall we had just been through and stopped in front of Chapin's door and knocked. Across the hall, another door flew open.

"You knocking again? He ain't there," said a fat redhead, a woman ten years too old for the braless knit shirt she had on. "So you might's well give up. Oh, it's you, Charlie." Her broad nostrils flared. "I ain't heard him for two, three days, now."

Charlie turned a sharp brown eye on Pedersen, that asked as clearly as any words how Pedersen had gotten into the building to knock on the door before him. But his mouth didn't ask, and he opened the door.

I didn't want to go in. I knew that smell. I'd caught a whiff of it before, out in the hall: the sweet, perversely tantalizing odor of spoiled meat, like the inside of a broken-down refrigerator. But Charlie and Pedersen eased into the room and I had to follow.

Chapin had had one of the efficiency

apartments. Good building in a good location, and a view, but not too much rent for a single man with a good job. He'd furnished it nicely, no flash, good taste, nothing out of line: prints on the wall, not Picasso originals, J. C. Penny polyester drapes across the wide window, not the Haitian cotton Karen was always drooling at in magazines. I kept my eyes away from the couch after the first glance.

"Oh, Jesus, the poor devil," Charlie said. "Think of that!"

"Maybe we should call the police," I said.

"Definitely call the police," Pedersen agreed. "Open your eyes, Jamison. He's been shot."

In the doorway behind us, the fat redhead started to scream.

Charlie got the redhead out of the way and the door locked and took us down to his lair to call the cops. While we waited, he produced some reasonable coffee, though I had to drink it black. Old he might be, and skinny and short and dressed like a hick, but there was nothing wrong with his brain. He wasn't about to let us get away before the police had a crack at us, but he was nice about it, playing an old man's game of astonishment and helplessness. "As God's my witness!" he kept saying. "As God's my witness, I never!" What he meant was, You guys are my witnesses, try and get away and I'll have your scalps. To aid in the scalping, he got our names from our driver's licenses.

I had my own worries, still, but I could worry just as well in the super's tiny office as anywhere else. If Bill Chapin, who had only ferried a piece of equipment to L.A., had been shot, what did that mean for Karen and Joey? Worse, the super had a morning paper folded on the table, and around the edge of it in smallish, lowercase headlines I could read "found frozen" over a small story near the bottom of the page. Finally, it was too much: I turned the paper over. COUPLE FOUND FROZEN was the whole headline; my eye caught the word "UFO" in the story and I read the one paragraph: another pair of crazy old coots who thought UFOs were going to rise from Lake Superior's enormous depths and save the world from humanity had parked their car in the cold on a lookout, and the North Shore weather had finished them off. I didn't know whether to be relieved that they were none of the crazies I knew, or apprehensive – because if one couple can freeze in a car, so can another, UFO or no UFO. So had another, in fact, back in the fall. Also waiting for UFOs.

"Sure, go ahead, read my paper," Charlie said. "Keep your mind off things."

"No, that's OK." I saw Pedersen's eye on the paper; he must have noticed the headline, too, because he smiled at me faintly.

Finally, the right cars converged on the parking lot: a squad car first, then the blue van marked HENNEPIN COUNTY MOBILE CRIME UNIT, and a couple of plain sedans. Charlie got up to let the police in.

Dealing with the cops was like dealing with the cops always is: slow, because they're sticklers for detail; boring, because they're slow. The afternoon was half gone before we got back to the plant to report to R. Quentin.

He clasped his hands tightly on his desk and bit his lower lip. "Did you check to see what he might have had there about Aunt Yuk?" he asked in a tight voice.

Pedersen started. The idea evidently hadn't occurred to him, either. "We had the building superintendent with us," I said. "We couldn't go poking around with him looking over our shoulders, not once he'd seen that Bill was dead."

"Why didn't you go in first, by yourselves?"

Pedersen's eyes narrowed. "J.J. thought we ought to have a witness, in case anything was seriously wrong," he said.

"That was a half-ass idea, J.J."

I wasn't about to protest that the hall smelled bad and I had wanted neutral company. So I said nothing.

"So far," R. Quentin mused, "We are doing OK. So far. The stock's still steady, so no rumors have leaked. After that climb last fall, you'd expect it to be shaky, too. And now we have Aunt Yuk back and we can just send her out again. *Unless* Bill had something at home about this mess and the cops see it for what it is, in which case we are up shit creek. I counted on you to be nosier, J.J."

"They will find nothing," Pedersen said. "Someone had already searched the apartment quite thoroughly."

"Now you tell me." Burns twisted his hands together. "Why didn't you tell me before?"

"You didn't ask."

I hadn't noticed any evidence of search, but then I'd been looking at the other end of the room, where Bill had had only a dining table and four chairs overlooking the river. "We couldn't have sneaked in anyway," I said. "He had a deadbolt lock."

Burns glanced at his telephone. "Well, go on back to work and keep your mouths shut, and I'll get back to you when I've checked with headquarters. God, I'll be glad when

Kochel gets back and takes this mess off my hands."

"Surely, it's your mess?" Pedersen asked blandly.

"Not for one second more than I can help," Burns said. His voice was distant. "Have you two had lunch? You'd better go have lunch."

We walked back down the hall, with its familiar hums and machine noises. "Where shall we go?" Pedersen asked. "It seems to me that expense account should stand us to that new Vietnamese place, doesn't it to you?"

"No."

"We did miss lunch on company business," Pedersen pointed out. "The cafeteria's closed at this hour, and you did hear our supervisor instruct us to go have lunch. And the expense account may not last much longer," he added wistfully.

"Lars, you're too much for me. I'm just going to run across the road and pick up an Arby's and eat it at my desk."

In the end, that's what Pedersen did, too.

Chapter Seven

The Twin Cities don't roll up their sidewalks on Friday nights. Plays, concerts, nightclubs, restaurants, ball games, bars topless or stodgy, you name it, it's all there, along with sundry less respectable entertainments. But a guy whose wife and small son have been missing for two days doesn't feel like partaking of any of it.

With Karen not at home, the grocery shopping hadn't been done. On the other hand, I'd been too upset to eat much, so it all evened out. I scrambled some eggs and ran half a bag of frozen french fries through the microwave, and poured ketchup over the whole pale, soggy mess when I remembered that I ought to eat a vegetable. That was dinner. I wanted company. Oh, I wanted company! Specifically, Karen's and Joey's company, but failing that, anybody else – only Mrs. Eskew's house had been dark all week, the Dixons were giving a party I hadn't been invited to and wasn't about to crash, and of all the guys I know at work, now that Bill Chapin was dead I was the only one who hadn't bought a house in the far suburbs.

I carried my plate into the living room and stood at the window looking out as I ate, with only the light that spilled out of the kitchen. Candy LeFleur's porch light was on, and her front windows glowed, but even in my lonely state I didn't have much use for Candy LeFleur, who not only pretended to be *authentique* French, although her name didn't even have the right definite article, but made nasty comments about my hobbies to the police.

The ghostly lights of a jet flying just above the cloud base on its approach to the airport moved toward me. As the roar passed over the house I thought of the people behind the row of windows, cigarettes extinguished and seatbacks in the upright position. None of them coming to me. None of them even thinking of talking to me.

That left me with my own mind, which I was tired of, and the TV. I dropped my dirty plate into the kitchen sink, and had just turned the boob tube on and settled down in my reclining chair when the telephone rang. I was astounded at the way my nostrils closed and my heart thumped as I went into the kitchen to answer it.

"Hi, J.J. It's Mack."

"Mack! Oh, jeeze, Mack! Why the hell didn't I think of you before? Mack, you're just the guy I need, and do I ever need you."

"What's up?"

Good old Mack. Whatever he'd called about, it sure wasn't Karen, but here he was ready to listen. We grew up in each other's pockets, Mack and I: same street, same schools, same peewee hockey and Little League teams. By high school we were finishing each other's sentences, falling over each other's words. We weren't as close, now: we'd both gone to the University of Minnesota, but I'd majored in computer science and become an engineer. Mack's no logician. What he's good at is people, and after a flirt with law school, he'd turned into a cop. I'd trust Mack with my life, or Karen's, or Joey's, without a second thought, and Mack – well, Mack would trust me with his, as long as it wasn't police business and he couldn't find another cop. Say Mack would trust my intentions.

"Mack, I think Karen's been kidnapped."

"You think! You don't know?"

"Well, I'm pretty sure. I got this call at work that was kind of – well, it's hard to explain, but she's gone, and Joey's gone, too."

"Slow down, J.J.," Mack said, slowly and

distinctly, the way he might tell somebody to drop the gun and put his hands over his head. Let's start over. First, have you called the Minneapolis police?"

"Yeah, but, see, there's this book she wanted me to notice and she called me J.J., you know she never called me J.J. in her life, Mack, but the cops here won't –"

"Whoa, whoa, whoa. You lost me on the first turn."

"Could you come over?"

"Not now. I'm on." I had a brief vision of Mack leaning over a desk in the police station out in St. Louis Park, the phone at his ear and activity all around him. Friday night. Friday nights are bad, he'd said a dozen times. "But I can give you a couple of minutes, anyway. Start at the beginning. You called the police. When?"

"Wednesday night."

"Wednesday night," he repeated, slow and calm again. "So she's been gone since Wednesday night?"

"Afternoon, I think. See, this jerk woman across the street from us –"

"Sit down, J.J. And talks slower." I don't know how he knew I was standing up, but I twirled one of the kitchen chairs to face me and sat on it. "What was the very first thing you knew?" Mack asked.

So I told him the story: Karen's call to me at work, me noticing that she'd used a different name, "Only not until after she hung up, damn it! I couldn't even ask her what was wrong!"

"Sure," Mack soothed. I went on: the mystery novel she'd called my attention to, the detective from Minneapolis who'd seemed so unimpressed, the whispery call at work. By that time, I was almost logical myself.

"That's the last thing you heard, then, that call that asked you to drop your investigation. Yesterday, right?"

I told him what I thought of the Minneapolis detective.

Cops are loyal to cops. He might be on a different force, but Mack said, "J.J., you got to remember, he doesn't know you from Adam. Now, you go to him with this wishy-washy story – and I'm not saying I don't believe it, I believe every word, but see, I know you, I know you're not just getting your own back when your wife walks out, see – and the only witness he's got besides you says your kid was laughing and your wife didn't seem upset when she left with this guy. Well, what would you think?"

I suggested a few things the Minneapolis detective could do with his spare time.

"I know, I know. What's this investigation?"

Oh, hell, how had I let that out? I leaned my elbows on my knees and my chin on the mouthpiece of the telephone, trying to think.

"J.J., you still there?"

"Yeah. Mack, this is something to do with work, and they don't want to let it out. Forget I said anything about any investigation."

"Sure. What did you tell the Minneapolis department, or is that top secret, too?"

"Don't get mad at me, Mack, please. I told them the guy called, but I said he said he'd arrange a ransom drop later."

"Well, you know what that's gonna look like to your detective, don't you?" Mack demanded.

"Yeah, he told me."

"Whose bright idea was it, anyway?"

"Belongs to my boss." I sighed. "Look, Mack, I'm really on the hook. If I let out that there was, uh, a need for this investigation, even just the need, it could look pretty bad for the company. We could lose contracts, people would get laid off. And for sure I'd be out of a job and I can tell you my references wouldn't be glowing, except maybe red. So what the hell can I do? And another thing."

I told him about Bill Chapin.

Silence for about thirty seconds. A long sigh. "I don't know, J.J. You really got yourself in a fuck-up this time. And you were always supposed to be the smartest kid in the class. How do you manage it?"

"Lay off, Mack. I don't know how I got in. I just want out."

"That's what they all say." Mack paused. "Look, I'll do what I can. I know a couple of guys that work in your precinct. I can maybe give you what-d'you-call-it. Character reference. That's about it, though."

"Thanks."

"Do yourself a favor, huh? Call that guy that has your case and tell him what you just told me."

"I'll think about it." I remembered that Mack had called me, not the other way around, however much sense it would have made. "What was it you called about?"

"Oh, I got something here looks like it might be up your alley. A UFO thing. No big rush."

I swallowed several naughty words: Mack couldn't know what a nerve he'd just touched. "That's okay. Shoot."

"Thanks. I got a lady here a while ago with a funny complaint. Seems her father's been hot the past few years on what she calls

'Fortean phenomena.' You ever heard of that?"

"Oh, one of those." I sighed. "Yeah. There was a guy named Charles Fort, he's been dead about fifty years, but he used to collect little stories about weird things. Monsters, blood falling out of the sky, people burning up for no reason, and so on. There's a type that goes google-eyed over them. Ancient astronauts kind of thing."

"Well, this is a little different," Mack said. "Seems there's some character going around with something that sounds a little like a religious cult. The general idea is that the UFOs have been sent to Earth to check out whether anybody here is good enough to take home with them."

"I've heard that one before."

"Have you really? I missed it. Well, this guy says it's all in the Bible," Mack went on, in a marveling tone of voice: Father Ambrose never put that in his catechism, you know it. "He says Jesus Christ came to Earth to tell people how to get ready to go away in a UFO. I bet you never heard that before."

"Sure I have," I said wearily. "It's old stuff, Mack."

"Okay, here's a new twist. This guy says you have to get rid of all your earthly wealth before you'll be eligible for the ride. You want chapter and verse?"

Matthew 19:21 through 30, I thought. "Not really."

"It's that stuff about the rich shall not enter the Kingdom of Heaven," Mack said. Right. "And this guy who's been talking to the lady's father is kind enough to help people out with getting rid of all their earthly possessions."

I'd heard that one before, too, of course, but there comes a point with Mack where it doesn't pay to be too know-it-all.

"Anyway, this guy is putting a big push on the lady's father to get all his stuff turned into money in the next few days and hand it over. By Wednesday, I think. The old guy is beside himself because he knows he can't sell his house by then, not with the market the way it is, and he wants to sign it over to his daughter and she can give him everything she's got saved. She listened for about two minutes and since she's got a little more on the ball than her old man, she hightailed it over here. I wondered if you'd heard anything like this."

"Not fresh, Mack, no. And not in this area. West of here, I think, two or three years ago. I don't know what finally came of it."

"The things people think up to part other

people from their money," Mack marveled. "Never ceases to amaze me. Sometimes I think some people oughta just pin a sign on their back, 'Rip me off.' Anyway, this time the daughter has a name for us. Sergeant Hawley. Ever heard of him?"

Sergeant Hawley. Not from the Salvation Army, for sure. "I don't think so. Sergeant of what?"

"Sergeant, that's his name. Smart parents, what if he'd joined the army and made colonel, how would that sound? Anyway, that's the name he's using; ten to one his parents never heard of it. But could you keep your ears open for me, J.J.?"

"Glad to."

"Thanks, old buddy. And I'll see what I can do about . . . about that other thing. J.J.?" Suddenly intense. "Keep me posted on that, huh?"

As near as Mack would ever come to saying he was worried. I promised I would, promised to stay cool, and hung up. Solid pal that he was, Mack had given me something to keep my mind busy. I went down to the basement and tried not to look at Joey's toys as I crossed to the filing cabinets I'd moved down there when my old office turned into Joey's room. It took me half an hour to make a short list of names, people who belonged to what I call the fan clubs, little groups that meet once in a while to trade whoppers about UFOs. Most of them aren't too friendly toward people like me, who turn their favorite tall tales into hoaxes or mistakes, but these few were the ones that seemed reasonably balanced, even to me.

Back upstairs, I tried calling the ones who lived closest, but either they were all out partaking of the joys of concerts, plays, restaurants, bars, movies, ball games and/or neighborhood parties, or the UFO had finally landed.

Lying awake in bed, I could see what Karen meant. The house made noises, the kind of noises I'd blame on the cat, if we had a cat, and they kept jerking me awake. At least I could sleep late, I comforted myself: but I woke early and reached for Karen. The cold sheet I found instead brought me fully awake, and although I tried every trick I'd ever heard of, I couldn't get back to sleep. When I turned on the yard light, thousands of tiny snowflakes glittered back at me, innocently adding to the layer I'd failed to shovel off our walks. Mindful of Minneapolis's snow removal ordinance, I got dressed and went out and scraped down to the concrete with my big blue scoop. The kid

Mrs. Eskew pays to do her walks had taken a vacation, so I did those, too. But it didn't help: my mind still burned with worry.

As of three-thirty that afternoon, give or take a few minutes, Karen and Joey would have been gone three days. The guy had telephoned. A kid had been crying. I began to hope the kid was Joey, because that might mean that the telephone had been indoors, and that might mean that the place had been heated, and that might mean that Karen and Joey were still warm, still OK, only tired and scared. I took the paper from the paper boy and put the shovel away. Then I went indoors and finished up the last of the shredded wheat, dry because I hadn't remembered to buy milk, and drank a cup of tea. Seven-thirty. The Tom Thumb over on 43rd would be ready to sell me all the milk I wanted, but I didn't dare walk over there because I'd just had a new thought: what if Karen got to a telephone? What if she had one and only one chance to call, and nobody was home?

What if she had called when I was on my way to work, or coming home? What if she'd called while I was out shoveling the damn snow? What if? What if, what if?

I identified the tapping sound I'd been half-hearing for the last three or four minutes as a chickadee at the window, come to nag me over the empty bird feeder. Birdseed I had; I went out and filled the feeder, but I left the door wide open, just in case the minute it took was *the* minute.

When I came in, I turned on the TV and watched cartoons.

Around ten-thirty the phone rang, a friend of Karen's. I put the woman off indefinitely, but the call reminded me of my project of the night before; I decided to give Karen's resourcefulness the benefit of the doubt and got out my list of semisane people to call.

Third time lucky.

"Sure, I've heard of Sergeant Hawley," said my "fan." "He's been around since last fall. Don't trust him, though."

"How come?"

"First rule of survival." He chuckled. "Never trust what a man says when he stands to make a lot of money out of it. Now, I appreciate that people like yourself think I'm a fool to spend so much time making lists of UFOs you think are nothing, but I'm not a damn fool, like some I could mention."

"People who gave Hawley money, you mean?"

He paused for a minute. "I'm not sure if anybody's given him any money yet."

"I hear he's putting deadlines on people," I said cautiously. The sun shone through the kitchen window for all of three seconds, and lit the dull red of a cardinal that had found the seed I'd put out.

"I don't know where you hear that," my fan said, equally cautiously. "Though I'm not saying it can't be so."

"What would you think of an old man who wanted so bad to sell his house by the middle of next week that he tries to sign it over to his daughter and get her to give him her savings?" I asked.

"I say he'd better have a good daughter. Not like some, who'd throw their own dads out on the street. Or that's where he'd end up."

"If I say Hawley had something to do with it?"

My fan took awhile to think it over. "Doesn't sound like Hawley, somehow. His big thing is purification by fire."

"His name was given. You want to put a stop to that kind of thing?"

Another long pause. "What you got in mind?"

I told him about Mack, gave him Mack's phone number, and told him it was up to him whether he made a call or not.

"I'll think it over. Want me to pass it around?"

"Whatever." Worst that could happen, I figured, was that Hawley would split before he got his hands on the cash and set up operations somewhere else. I picked another number, belonging to a member of a different fan club, and tried again. This one was, well, unreceptive. I told him not to take any wooden nickels and hung up.

By noon, I'd finished the calls. I had three maybes for Mack, and I figured I'd done what I could for the time being, small as it was.

I don't know what Mack did with his Saturday morning, but some of it must have been working on his end of our bargain, because while I was assaulting my stomach with my fourth cup of black coffee in lieu of lunch, the hairy detective pounded on my door.

"Oh, you again," I said graciously.

"Got any more coffee?"

I shrugged and led the way into the kitchen, poured the dregs of the pot into a mug, and handed it to him. He reversed one of the kitchen chairs and sat on it with his arms folded across the top. "I've heard some more on your wife."

Suddenly, I was having trouble breathing.

"I've heard you two get along well. I've heard that you *usually*" – he lingered over the word – "can be depended upon to be accurate. So I'm ready to dig harder."

"You've been talking to Mackenzie Forrester."

The detective grinned. "Let's just say, a friend of a friend. And let me correct an impression you may have, Mr. Jamison. I haven't just sat on this. I've been through the neighborhood looking for witnesses. I've checked every report that might have had anything to do with either your wife or your son, I've put out an alert in case they are seen. But it's a bad-luck case. Like, your neighborhood nosey wasn't home, hasn't been since."

"Mrs. Eskew?"

"Next door, right. The only person who saw your wife and son with this person is the lady across the street, and to be frank with you, Mr. Jamison, she's a better talker than she is a watcher."

I sighed. "I know."

"Now, you want to tell me *all* about it?"

I leaned against the counter with my arms folded and stared at the floor. Under the edge of the stove I could see a couple of dried-up splashes of coffee I'd missed the night before last. "I'm in a bad spot," I said.

"If I tell you everything I know, I get a lot of other people in trouble and maybe lose my job. If I were a genius, that might not matter, but I'm just a run-of-the-mill engineer, and a bad reference could give me a hard time getting a new job. Only I want my wife and kids."

The guy nodded and sat on my kitchen chair with his arms folded, and after a couple of minutes he lowered his chin onto his forearms.

I sighed. "OK, I'll tell you the outline. If it's not enough, ask, and maybe I can tell you more. But keep as much of it to yourself as you can, OK?"

He gestured, hands empty. "I'm not writing it down."

He had brown eyes, with lids that hung a little heavily over the iris, giving him a sleepy, half-stupid look, but I didn't for a minute think that anything I said would go in one ear and out the other without leaving some kind of trace. I sighed again.

"Here goes. A very expensive gadget went missing from my company on a flight to the west coast. I don't suppose you get many cases of industrial espionage in this precinct, but that was the first thing on everybody's mind when Aunt – when this thing disappeared. Only you don't just call in the cops for that, not until you've got pretty good evidence of what's happened, because then the company loses contracts, the stock goes down, people get laid off, so on and so on. In times like these, it's worse."

"So who looks for your gadget?"

"In this case, for a little while, me. And another guy I work with. I know it sounds crazy, but if you knew the way my boss's mind works, it wouldn't. See, this other guy and I had worked on this thing, so we knew what we were looking for, and the other guy ... has some talents that might come in handy in a case like this." I thought I had phrased that rather neatly. "And I have a reputation, entirely undeserved, as an investigator, because – hold onto your hat – I work for an organization that investigates UFO sightings."

"Oh," the detective said. "You *are* that Jamison."

"Yeah, that one. In fact, I got in on this late because I was out in North Dakota telling some kid it wasn't nice to play with shiny silver balloons quite the way he did."

"Just balloons, huh?"

"Just balloons. The stringer for the *National Enquirer* like to cried."

"He recovered quick enough. The story

was in the *Tribune* Monday, complete with snapshot. Nothing about balloons, though."

"That so?" I'd been driving back, somewhere near the Minnesota border when the paper came out, so I hadn't seen it. "Anyway, when I got back, this other guy and I did what we could, which was practically zero, and then the next day this happened."

"Your wife disappearing."

"Yeah. And then the guy called Thursday morning and said my wife and son were OK and they wouldn't be harmed, if I put off the investigation ten more days."

"Um." The detective looked almost asleep. "What would that do?"

"Well, at the time I thought it would give somebody time to take this, uh, gadget apart and see how it works."

"But?"

"We found it. That is, it was found, in Los Angeles. Apparently it never left the airport, it was just misplaced somehow."

"Shipped by air." The guy nodded, still looking sleepy, the tip of his tongue pressed against his upper teeth. Outlining it all in what passed for his mind. I wanted to paste him one, for making me doubt Karen, but he was on my side, now – maybe he'd always been – so I just slumped against the counter and waited.

"Can you make sense of that? I can't."

"No. And there's more. The guy who was escorting this, uh, object, got shot."

The bushy eyebrows rocketed upward. "When was that?"

"I don't know. This other guy and I found him in his apartment yesterday morning. He hadn't been in for three days, and we went to check on him. Lived in one of those new buildings on the bluff, by the river."

"I think I saw the bulletins on that," the detective said, staring out the window. "Yeah. Chapin? Nothing about this episode you're being so cagey about."

"I told you about that. What goes for me goes double for him, and double that for our boss."

The hairy detective thought it over for several minutes. "What can you tell me about this guy's apartment? The one that got shot?"

"Damn all. It's only one room, but I was too busy not looking at Bill to notice anything besides his drapes."

The man took a deep breath and let it out slowly, then got up and spun the chair to face the table and encouraged it back into place with the palm of his hand, the way he might shoo a small child. "I don't like that at all," he said. He gazed steadily at one corner of the kitchen ceiling, until I glanced up to see if I'd missed some more splashes of coffee. The corner was clean. "I guess you don't like it, either," he said. "Well, at least now I know why your boss is so worried about this hitting the newspaper. I'll keep you posted."

He was out the door before I had sorted that last bit out. Trust Burns to put the company first.

Celia Dixon called a little later and offered to do some shopping for me, and I took her up on it. That was the extent of the excitement for the day. Even with the football playoffs on television, it was a long, long Saturday afternoon, and an even longer evening.

Purely my fault. I noticed the corner of a piece of paper sticking out under the cover of Karen's typewriter and pulled it out to see if she had left me some kind of clue. What I found was the rough draft of a story about a woman who finally left her husband because he was away so often, a week at a time. The guy in the story spent all his time in Detroit, installing and testing computer systems in a car factory, but I'm not terminally stupid.

Sunday also dragged. Word of Karen's disappearance was slowly spreading, thanks to Celia and Candy LeFleur. I got calls from a bunch of people, including Pedersen, expressing concern or looking for news, or both. Mack dropped by with a telephone answering machine, all on his own, and once he'd shown me how to set it up we split a six-pack over the first half of that afternoon's football game. When we ran out of beer, Mack went home. He's starting a pot, Mack is. I guess we're none of us getting any younger.

Monday morning I got myself shaved and dressed, and stood at the window in the family room, looking past the snow that had sifted through the screens of the back porch. Out in the yard I'd installed a swing set the summer before. The seats of the swings were rounded with snow, the end of the slide buried. Should I go to work? Stay home?

Even Karen would expect to find me at work on a Monday morning. I set up the answering machine, checked my forlorn little note on the kitchen table, added a second row of hearts at the top, and to work I went. I was a few minutes early, in fact, but there was already a pink note on my desk: See Bob Burns. What could R. Quentin want now, I wondered. He had his gizmo back. I reminded myself that I did have a job and

Burns was my boss, and trotted obediently down the hall.

"Come in," R. Quentin said. "Sit down."

He was a lot more somber than I liked. I pulled up a chair and perched on the edge of it with a flutter of apprehension, while Burns stared out his window.

"Aunt Yuk's been cut," he said.

I felt my jaw settle downward. So. Someone had taken the gadget apart, just as Pedersen had anticipated, and put her back together well enough to pass a cursory inspection. Not in any baggage room in the L.A. airport, either. "How do you know?"

"Hardware checked her out. Couple of sloppy wire wraps, specks of solder. A garage job," he added contemptuously.

He didn't mean that it had literally been done in a garage. Just that someone without the manufacturing facilities our own engineers enjoy had done the dirty work. "Has anyone come peddling, do you know?" I asked.

"Not to us, naturally." Burns was playing with his pen, a plain black plastic shaft emblazoned with the company logo, leaving little black dots on his desk blotter as he pushed down on it, turned it end for end, pushed down again. He looked down at his bunched fingers. "Somebody in this unit is a spy, J.J."

"Does it have to be this unit? A lot of people knew what we were working on."

"Nobody knew Chapin was traveling. Not even headquarters."

"Couldn't somebody have called, been told he was gone for the next few days. . . ."

"Wilmot says no." Mike Wilmot shared Chapin's cubicle, and hence his telephone. But Wilmot wouldn't have stayed in the cubicle every working minute. He'd get coffee, go to the john, have lunch, like anybody else, even if he didn't have any reason to go down to the computer room.

R. Quentin Burns was way ahead of me. "And Lisa hasn't listed any calls on her line," he added. After six rings, calls automatically transfer to the unit secretary's desk, and she keeps a running log of times and people called.

"Chapin could have told someone. A girl, a neighbor . . ."

"Mata Hari?" Burns snorted. "Not likely, is it? Headquarters has had a talk with the company shrink," he added. "We have a behavior profile he gave us, to check everyone against. Little changes, the kind of nerves a person would get, sitting on fifteen or twenty K."

I hadn't seen everyone in the unit since coming back from North Dakota. There are a couple of dozen of us, counting technicians. Other than Chapin, who didn't usually get shot, I hadn't noticed any unusual behavior, but why should I?

"That person might not follow his usual routine, come in funny times, might avoid having lunch with coworkers, talk less or more than usual, show different patterns of interests. . . ." R. Quentin sort of trailed off, uncharacteristic verbal behavior for him. He'd been my boss almost six years, and I knew his speech habits well.

"Sounds reasonable," I said.

The pen jerked out of his fingers onto the floor, and he leaned down to pick it up. "Are you sure you don't know where your wife is?" he asked, his voice muffled by the desk and carpet. "You're sure she hasn't just packed up and gone to stay with a friend? Because you're the only one who fits the profile, J.J., and you're also smart enough to manufacture a problem to use as camouflage."

Speechless, I stared at him as he sat up in his chair again. He wouldn't meet my eyes.

"You're sure you were really in North Dakota?" he went on. "Not out in L.A., doing a little intercepting?"

"I – I handed out a lot of business cards, I – it was in the paper Monday, I –"

"You could have had a friend hand out the cards," he said. "The picture was just a distance shot. You've been with the company a long time, J.J. I'd hate to think you'd done anything foolish. I was going to put you up for a grade promotion on this next salary review."

More money and more responsibility, a trade-off that would normally have filled me with a mixture of elation and apprehension, but now the idea fell flat. Bulldozed by suspicion. "She's really gone," I said, choking over the anger beginning to rise. "I don't know where." I got up and stamped out of the office, although R. Quentin hadn't said the meeting was over. He didn't call me back.

Pedersen wasn't in our cubicle when I reached it. I sat down at my desk and clenched my fists in my lap and thought about writing a letter of resignation. Then I unclenched my fists and pulled out a pad of quadrille paper and began writing.

Pedersen ambled in with a cup of coffee in each hand and blandly read my letter over my shoulder. "That's somewhat premature, isn't it?" he asked.

"The bastard thinks I stole Aunt Yuk,"

I said through my teeth. "He thinks I sent Karen and Joey home to mother to cover my nerves if they showed. He keeps dangling good salary reviews and bad salary reviews in front of my nose, as if all I cared about the job was how much money I could get out of it, and –"

"All valid grievances," Pedersen agreed. "Still, I would miss you when you were no longer sitting there interfering with my free use of the terminal. If your complaints begin to rankle too greatly, why not go to Kochel?"

"He's still on vacation." Not a bad idea, though: Kochel, already a step over Burns, was a good-buddy guy who'd been project engineer on the last thing I'd done, and I knew him pretty well.

"Put the letter in your desk, and if in a week you still feel the same way, then send it," Pedersen advised. "That's what I have always done, and the letter has never been sent."

I turned and gaped at him, but he just set one of the cups down on my desk and carried the other to his own. "Rage is seldom constructive until it is controlled," Pedersen said. "One of the few maxims of my mother's I have adopted." I couldn't imagine Pedersen enraged, even under control, but maybe that just showed how good he was at controlling it.

"I, for example, in just this past week have refrained on many occasions from flinging this terminal over this partition, perhaps to visit five kilos of destruction upon an innocent skull – that despite its reluctance to provide me with information about Mr. Leonard Fink. Instead, I turned my emotion inward to stimulate my brain, and have won, only this morning, that most singular of prizes, his Social Security number. It is the key to everything." Pedersen smirked. "Worth making a trek to the cafeteria to treat us to some reasonable version of coffee."

Good grief! "Thank you," I managed. "Congratulations."

Pedersen took his bows and applied himself once more to the computer. I finished my letter of resignation, left it unsigned, and put it in my center desk drawer for future reference. Then I went back to work on the bane of my existence, documenting a complicated program.

It was slow work, and I was glad when Pedersen suggested we break for lunch together. He took the phone off the computer's cradle and returned it to its normal rest, and we began bundling up against the mild Minnesota winter. I was just about to walk out when the telephone rang.

"Jamison?"

The whisperer. I felt my heart begin to thud.

"I warned you not to continue your investigation. I have ways of knowing whether you have or not. I find you have."

My eyes strayed to the terminal Pedersen had been giving such heavy use.

"One more chance," the whisperer continued. My heart skipped a beat. "I suggest you take it. You know what can happen now, don't you?"

Chapin, for example, was dead. "Where's my wife? Can I talk to her?" I asked hurriedly, but the whisperer had already hung up.

After a moment I put the phone down and unbuttoned my overcoat. "I'm sorry, Lars," I said. "All of a sudden, I'm not very hungry."

"Another call about Karen?"

I nodded.

Pedersen pulled at his chin. "Just a moment," he said, and crossed to the phone. He dialed and waited. "May I speak to Basil Devitt?" he asked. "Oh, no? . . . Can you tell me when he's expected? . . . Thank you very much." He hung up. "Devitt's gone to lunch," he said. "But there are plenty of phones at the airport."

Devitt. Tanned and fit, tall enough to be described that way, who played raquetball when other men's wives disappeared. A cramp of anger hit my belly. Still hunched in my overcoat, I dialed the detective in charge of Karen's case.

"No ransom demand?" he demanded.

"No. Same as before. Only he also said, you know what can happen. I guess" – my throat tightened, and my voice went high – "I guess he meant Bill Chapin –"

"Take it easy, Mr. Jamison," the blurry voice soothed. "We've got no evidence of anything of the kind, so far. Try to put it out of your mind, if you can. We're doing everything possible."

Nothing, in other words. I was feeling nasty. "Have you checked out Basil Devitt?" I asked.

"Who's he?"

"President of Budjetair, the line the gadget was flying on. The only person outside the company – besides you – who knew an investigation was going on."

"I can't check things I don't know about," the detective protested. "Try to remember to tell me what you want me to know, huh?"

Fair enough, I guessed. "Well, I told you."

"I'll get on it."

"Thanks," I said, and hung up.

Pedersen was still standing in the doorway. "Shall I come with you to see Burns?" he offered.

"No, thanks. I'll do it myself." I stormed down the hall and flung open R. Quentin's door without knocking.

"I just had another call," I announced, without going into the room. My knees were shaking, I noticed with an odd sense of detachment. "The same as before. Call off the investigation, or something will happen to Karen and Joey. Like happened to Bill Chapin."

Robert Quentin Burns looked me straight in the eye, his mouth a thin, white, hostile line. "You're lying," he snapped. "Get out of here before I fire you, J.J."

I tried to slam the door, but the construction's too chintzy to get a satisfying bang, so I had to be content with stomping back to my cubicle, my galoshes rattling ludicrously. I yanked open the center drawer of my desk and grabbed for my letter of resignation.

It was gone, of course. In its place was a

triangular scrap torn from a piece of printout. "Patience," it said, in Pedersen's elegant European scrawl.

Chapter Eight

As I was about to leave that evening, Mike Wilmot caught up with me and invited me to have a drink with him in the bar across the road. The idea of standing with my elbow on the bar dissecting yesterday's football game didn't appeal to me, and I started to phrase a refusal.

"Please, J.J. I've got to talk to you." He glanced at the guard behind the desk. "About Bill Chapin."

At that, I nodded.

We were a little late leaving, so the bar was already crowded when we entered. I saw a few people I knew, none of them much of a surprise. The bar was the kind with lamps made out of the hubs of old carriage wheels, lots of dark oak paneling, red-plaid walls, and drinks sold at a 500-percent profit, features the customers seemed prepared to accept, even the last one.

"Look," Wilmot said, when he'd been furnished with a double Scotch on the rocks, and I had a mug of beer in one hand. "I'll get straight to the point. You were with Lars when he found Bill. Did it look like suicide to you?"

"Suicide?" I closed my eyes briefly to keep my head from spinning. "I didn't see him, so I don't know. But it doesn't sound like Bill to kill himself, does it?"

"How could you not see him?" Wilmot demanded, agitated. "He's only got one room. He told me so himself. It was the only way he could afford to live in that building."

"I didn't look."

Wilmot squeezed his eyes shut. "I guess I can see that. Oh, Jesus, I wish I knew what to do. I wish you had more guts, J.J."

"What gave you the idea it was suicide?"

"Didn't you see the paper?"

We spent a few minutes attracting the bartender's attention and a couple more borrowing a *Star and Tribune* from him. Wilmot paged through the Metro section looking for the paragraph he'd read that morning. "Here it is."

Sure enough.

> The death of William Chapin, discovered in his apartment in the Bluff Towers building on Friday morning by co-workers concerned over his absence from his job, is being treated initially as suicide, according to the Hennepin County Medical Examiner's office. Chapin

is reported to have been despondent over recent professional reverses.

"I guess it could be," I said uneasily. The sheriff's office had been there, with their Mobile Crime Unit, and they knew more about that kind of thing than I did.

"Yeah, but if that's right, then why did he change his mind? Monday afternoon he was mad as hell over losing Aunt Yuk, but he wasn't, what did they say, despondent. He was talking about taking Tuesday off to try to get to the bottom of the business."

"That sounds a lot more like Bill," I agreed.

"See, I think he did find something," Mike Wilmot said. He leaned closer. "I think he figured it out, and you know how Bill was, he'd have said right out he was going to report it to Burns, or maybe to Kochel when he gets back."

"Could be." I felt even chillier than the beer had left me. I could see Bill Chapin confronting whoever had made a fool of him, and he wouldn't have been pleasant about it.

"See, that's what I'm worried about," Wilmot said. "What if this guy gets the idea Bill told me who he is? What if I'm next?"

"Why should he tell you? Because you share an office?"

"That, yeah, and you remember I spent a lot of time helping him rewire that shack of his. People might think we were close pals, or something."

"Hell, Mike, everybody got roped into doing something on that place of his. I grouted the bathroom tile bare-handed, and my skin peeled off just like gloves the next day."

"And you aren't scared?"

"Not of that," I said. "Why not the guys on the three sides of you? You know how voices carry over those partitions. He'd have to whisper. Can you see Bill whispering?"

"There's that." Wilmot didn't look much comforted. "I guess nobody in his right mind would go in for wholesale slaughter over what, twenty, thirty thou?"

"No." I wasn't much comforted myself. If Chapin had killed himself, if the paragraph in the paper wasn't a mistake or a ruse, where did that leave me with Karen? And if he hadn't, I didn't want to think about that, either. "Look, Mike, I want to get home," I said. "If my wife can get near a telephone, that's where she'll call, and I don't want to miss it if I can help it."

"Oh, sure. I forgot about your wife,"

Wilmot said, still glum. "Good luck on that, J.J. See you tomorrow." He signaled the bartender, and by the time I'd threaded my way through a crowd already beginning to thin out, he was on one of the bar stools with another double.

I trudged through the dark parking lot and waited for the light to change, crossed the four lanes of the highway and took the walkway past the plant to get to my car. The minute I got home, I checked the answering machine: nobody there but Mack, and Mack was just checking. He thanked me for getting one of the fans to talk to him, complained that he wasn't any closer to his man, and wished me luck.

"Stay cool, J.J.," he signed off, and the tape clicked.

Stay cool. Not hard to do: the temperature had gone from a balmy 34° into the teens, and a soft snow was falling, the kind that looks like one of those old shake 'em up balls with a snowman in the bottom, the good kind, with glycerine to make the flakes sift down real slow.

I was watching the weatherman on the ten o'clock news brazenly forecasting more partly cloudy weather in spite of the stuff falling outside my window when the telephone rang.

"Hello, J.J., this is Prunella Watson," said the elderly voice I knew so well. "How are you?"

"Kind of tied up, to tell you the truth, Prue."

"Oh, dear." She did sound disappointed. "I had hoped you'd found time to investigate that last sighting by now."

"I did, Prue. I sent you the report right away."

"Oh, did you!" Glad relief. "Perhaps it's been delayed in the mail. The post office is so slow these days."

"It was only balloons."

"More balloons? Oh, dear."

The North Stars were winning a hockey game and the announcer was reporting that fact as if six of his sons were on the starting lineup. "*More* balloons? What do you mean, Prue? Have there been others?" I could just see myself with a new fad hoax, running back and forth like a kitten in a yard full of butterflies.

"Those ones in North Dakota just last week. I did get your report on that."

"Prue, we're at cross purposes," I said. "That's the last thing you asked me to check out, that thing in Bottineau."

"No, dear." She said it *deah,* no r. I'd visited Prunella Watson in Boston, once, and

I could picture her, a somewhat thin old woman with fluffy white hair and vague blue eyes, whose hands looked incomplete without some sort of garment twitching in a set of knitting needles. "I mean the one in Roseville. My map says Roseville is just north of St. Paul, so I thought it would be an easy one for you."

I turned my back on the television. "That's right, it's only about ten miles from me," I said. "But I haven't heard anything about a sighting in Roseville."

"You haven't?" She sounded even more disappointed. I wondered if her ginger cat were on her lap – she'd said once that petting a cat was a sure cure for a "turmoled mind" and had urged me to get one right away. I married Karen instead. "And it did sound like such a good one," she sighed. "The trail's a little cold by now."

Any trail in Roseville would be cold in January, I thought, but didn't say. Prunella doesn't appreciate flippancy. "It didn't make the news here, or at least I didn't hear it if it did. I don't know what you're talking about."

"I guess that means that nice man didn't get in touch with you, after all," she said. "And he sounded so very *dedicated!*"

"Prue, you'd better start at the beginning.

I'm – I'm a little upset about something, and I'm not following you very well. What man?"

"Oh, dear, is it a bad time?" she inquired anxiously. "I could call back later, if that would be better."

"No, it's fine, I want to hear about it. Only pretend I'm stupid, OK?"

Prue isn't one for cheap shots, either. "A man called me last Tuesday," the old voice said patiently, shifting into the mode she'd used for talking to kindergarten students for forty years, long before she'd organized CATCH. "He described a sighting in Roseville, Minnesota – mmm, I can give you the details. . . ." I heard her shifting papers.

"Don't bother with the details now," I said. "Why didn't you call me before? That's almost a week ago."

"Because the man who reported the sighting to me said he would call you. He said it would save the organization a little money, since he was right in your area. So I gave him your name and your phone numbers at work and at home – that was all right, wasn't it?" she asked, her voice sharp with worry.

"Sure, that's always OK, you know that." Tuesday. What was Tuesday? I'd gone out to Budjetair with Pedersen, had a mild argument with my wife, what else? Not much. "When on Tuesday?"

"Oh, around five."

Five Boston time is four in Minneapolis. Someone in too much of a hurry to wait for the rates to go down. "Did he leave you his name?"

"Yes. Just a minute. Here it is. John Ferraro."

"John Ferraro!" Ferraro is the head of a fan club that meets in Edina, not fifteen minutes' drive from my house. "Prue, that can't be. I know John Ferraro. I talked to him just last Saturday morning, and he didn't say one word about any sightings in Roseville or anywhere else except the one in Bottineau. He was all over me about that one."

"Is he a fan, or an investigator?" Prue inquired, severely.

"A fan, but he's not crazy."

"Still."

Still, he might not want me investigating something he'd turned up for himself. But then why call Prue? Or had he called her, and then changed his mind when he saw the thing in the paper from the day before? And why not just look in the phone book in the first place? "Prue, this is making zero sense.

What exactly did this guy say to you about the telephone number?"

"Just that he wanted to know who was investigator for that region, currently. He seemed to think it might have changed in the past couple of years," she said uncomfortably.

How recently had I talked to Ferraro, before last Saturday? A long time. Maybe not since the last local hoax I'd checked out, one with enough complications that a more sensible man would probably have resigned from CATCH on the spot. So he might have given me the benefit of the doubt.

"Something funny is going on here, Prue," I said finally. "You can give me the details on that sighting if you want, but I'm not sure it will accomplish anything."

I was wrong, as I so often am. As Prunella Watson's description progressed, it began to sound familiar. Very familiar. I couldn't quite pick it out from the hundreds of sightings I've heard described or read about in the last ten years, but I knew it had been based on one of them. After she finished, I went downstairs and started going through my files.

Hunting through paper is a lot slower than asking a computer to search its memory, and I regularly curse myself for not having a computer to store the CATCH records in. My files are cross-indexed, though, something Karen did for me in the far-off days of her enthusiasm, and this time the paper hunt cost me only fifteen minutes.

Four years earlier, in what had been described in the national press as "a suburb of Yankton, South Dakota" (a Missouri River valley town of all of 13,000 souls), a Yankton County deputy sheriff had given chase to "a small, brightly glowing ball of fire" (probably the planet Venus). Eyes on the sky and driving by the seat of his pants, he'd caught a raccoon just right and flipped his car into the ditch. The majority of the population of suburban Yankton is either four-legged or feathered, and took no notice of these antics.

Various featherless two-legged types had taken notice, however, and a small crowd had poked around where the car had broken the edge of the roadbed, congratulating each other on the deputy's good sense in not hitting a skunk. Among them was me. One or two of the others had wanted to be interviewed, but the rest of them were just figures, moving up and down the road or trespassing in the nearby fields or standing in a ring around us as I talked to one of the eager ones. Nameless people, most of them, people I'd thought I'd never see again.

But I had seen one of them again, just last Tuesday. Out at the airport. The man with the silver eyes. I hadn't been close enough then to see his face, but *now* I remembered that slightly scurrying gait, so unusual in a tall man.

I left a message with Joy Forrester for Mack to call me back when he got off duty and went to bed. The sixth night alone, but I slept a little better than I had since Friday morning's grim discovery, even though I owed Basil Devitt an apology.

Mack still hadn't called when I got up the next morning: he wouldn't, if he got back late and no one had told him it was a matter of life and death. When I went out to fetch the newspaper I found about four inches of partly cloudy covering my sidewalks. I said to hell with Minneapolis and its snow removal ordinance, left the partly cloudy where it was, and spread the paper out on the kitchen table.

It was Chapin I was interested in. I skipped past the headlines about Lebanon, unemployment, recession, and so forth, and concentrated on the little items, the ones that filled the ends of the columns and made a nice, neat frame for the ads. I'd barely started on my search when Mack called.

"Tell me what this Sergeant Hawley looks like," I said, after the requisite pleasantries.

"Why, you got a lead?"

"I've got something, maybe. First tell me what he looks like."

"I don't have much of a description, to tell you the truth," Mack said. "These people are pretty close-mouthed. I guess not even an idiot wants to look like an idiot."

"Tall? Skinny? Dark hair, light gray eyes?"

"I don't know about the eyes, but the rest fits," Mack acknowledged. "What's up?"

"He's got Karen."

Mack takes a lot of convincing, sometimes. I admit it was a big adjustment to make. I went through the whole thing: the guy at the airport sneaking around and attracting Pedersen's attention, Pedersen's joke –

"Why would he want to do a half-ass thing like that?" Mack wanted to know. "Sounds like about a fourth-grade trick."

"You're asking me? Just say, he's got a retarded sense of humor. Listen, will you?"

I told him about the call Prunella Watson had had, why it couldn't have been John Ferraro – I didn't mention his name – and that she'd given out my phone numbers.

"How would he know to call her?" Mack demanded.

"It was in the papers, Monday morning. That somebody from CATCH had investigated that hoax in North Dakota. It had my picture, and it gave the phone number of the national headquarters."

"National headquarters! You mean this is really a big outfit?"

"Don't get excited. It's only a little old lady who lives all by herself with her cat. I figure this Hawley guy must have remembered me from that thing in Yankton –"

I stopped and told him about the thing in Yankton. Mack had a good laugh at the deputy. I told him that if he had a dollar for every time Venus had been cleared to land at some airport, he could fly to Yankton and laugh in person.

"Anyway, after Pedersen had his little joke, Hawley thought I was investigating his racket. Only the only thing I was really investigating was this job for work, so naturally all this time I've thought that was what he was talking about."

"Right, I see that," Mack agreed. "But then why did this guy Chapin get himself killed?"

"Chapin might have killed himself," I

said. "I saw a thing in yesterday's paper about that."

"You guys take things awful hard," Mack commented. "Do yourself a favor and learn to relax, J.J."

"Sure. You want to hear where you come in, or are you gonna sit there and play shrink?" I waited out his protest. "See, I called a bunch of people for you, Saturday morning, remember? Those guys who called and talked to you were only three of them, the willing ones. One of the others must have told Hawley about it, and he figured I was still on his tail. So on Monday" – good Lord, only yesterday? – "he called me up and warned me again."

Silence. Then: "Jeez, J.J., I'm sorry."

"Well, how could you know?"

"I hope –" Mack apparently thought better of specifying what he hoped. "So Karen being kidnapped has nothing to do with your job."

"Not a damn thing. It's just a fluke." I wondered what I'd say to Pedersen. "So you see it, don't you? All you have to do is get Hawley, get him to tell you where Karen and Joey are."

Mack sighed heavily, a whistle in the telephone. "That's not going to be so simple, J.J. The guy's like a ghost, you reach for him and he disappears. We don't even know where to start looking."

"Can't you ask this woman whose father –"

"He shut up like a safe when he found out what she'd done. Nothing there. We've tried everything but gelignite to open him up."

I didn't say anything. I hadn't realized before how much hope I had pinned on the simple fact of knowing who knew where Karen and Joey were. Eyes clenched against tears, I took a deep breath and tried to unlock my throat.

"J.J.? You OK?"

I remembered something else, and my throat started working again. "He said, that first time, delay the investigation ten days, Mack. Six days are almost up. So he must be planning to collect in the next four days, right?"

"Check."

"And if he gets it, maybe he'll just turn them loose and get out with the cash, right?"

"Check," Mack said, with only the slightest hesitation: one split second that fueled every fear I had.

"Maybe one of my fans can tell us where they're supposed to turn over the money," I said.

"J.J., stay out of this. Just stay out," Mack

said. "I've got your three names, and I'll get back to them right away. Meanwhile, you'd better call the Minneapolis police and let them know what you've figured out. Give them my name, we can work together, check?"

"Sure," I said.

Mack reads minds. Mine, anyway. "You keep the hell out, check? And stay cool, fella."

"Sure."

Mack had two names. I had five or six others: John Ferraro for one. If I called him and told him his name had been used to get my phone number, and my wife and son had been kidnapped as a result, I was pretty sure he'd go along with what I wanted. I hung up on Mack and went back to the newspaper, looking for the item about Chapin I half-hoped was there, the one that would confirm his suicide.

Chapter Nine

Chapin wasn't mentioned anywhere in the paper. What I found was Wilmot.

I am blessed/cursed with a good visual imagination: a few sentences based on two interviews, three short paragraphs in the back of the newspaper, and I could see it all, like a movie running inside my head. And I'd been pushing down a lot of pictures lately, too many pictures: Karen and Joey unidentified in hospitals, or worse – jammed under the ice of the Mississippi, buried in snow and waiting for spring to exhume their bodies –

But Wilmot took me by surprise. I couldn't push him away.

I played it out in my mind, a movie unreeling: Wilmot finishes the second Scotch on the rocks quickly, not talking to anyone. The bartender is trying to keep an eye on him: the guy looks pale – "shocky," was what the barkeep said later – and he makes it a point to wipe the glossy mahogany in front of Wilmot's elbows often. Wilmot isn't exactly a stranger. He doesn't come in often, but when he does, he is likely to drink a little too much, and it's hard to tell whether this is a time he'll get woebegone, or belligerent. Woebegone, maybe: usually the short, stocky guy has a friend or two with him, but now he is alone.

Wilmot, half-aware of the hovering bartender because the man's red jacket keeps intruding on the edge of his vision, pays no attention. He holds his third glass of Scotch between his palms, swirling it from time to time and watching the ice melt into liquid curls in the liquor, making a conscious effort to slow down. That first drink had disappeared in a hell of a hurry, and he wasn't quite sure where the second had gone, either. It wouldn't be so great to get drunk, not if he's really in danger.

His mind wanders back to Bill Chapin. Could the guy really have killed himself? . . . J.J. was no help at all. Wilmot turns the suicide idea in his mind, examining it like a specimen encased in clear plastic, trying to fit it in with what he knows of his office mate. Impulsive, yes, Chapin could be impulsive. But it was always a . . . a . . . a selfish impulse, like selling that house he'd spent forever remodeling before he was even done with it and getting a hole of an apartment at a good address to impress some chick, or that time he'd traded in his Chevette on a big BMW cycle and then had had to trade back – to a lime-green Fiat – when cold weather arrived. Good clothes and a good dinner, and NSP on his back about the electric bill. It doesn't fit with suicide, Wilmot decides. But then what?

Hell with it. Wilmot tosses off the rest of the drink and orders another, a single this time, annoyed when the bartender is slow serving him. He isn't drunk, damn it, doesn't even have that funny tingle just under his nose he takes as a warning. When the drink finally comes, he again warms it in his hands. But even a few handfuls of peanuts and pretzels don't help him slow down: the drink is inside his belly in under ten minutes. Wilmot gets carefully down from the bar stool and shrugs his down jacket up onto his shoulders, pleased with himself for remembering that it is January, cold out. His car, a year-old Escort that Chapin had sneered at, is across the highway in the company lot, and while the weather is still extraordinarily warm for January, the chill hits him as he walks out of the bar.

He stops to zip his jacket and pull the collar up around his ears. The sound of a motor revving nearby makes him wish he'd brought his car across. But J.J. had wanted to walk, and Wilmot hadn't been willing to look any softer than he had to, not with the running-scared questions he was planning to ask. He frowns, balancing himself against the brisk southerly wind. Had he asked all the questions? He has a hazy idea of something further he should have done, should have thought of, but it's gone, floating away on the warm surface of the Scotch.

Wilmot steps out into the cleared part of the bar's narrow parking lot, watching for cars turning in from the highway with the exaggerated concentration of a man who is drunker than he thinks he is. He pays no attention to the rough-running engine behind him, to the lights coming up and shooting his shadow at the mounds of plowed-up snow at the end of the lot. He doesn't hear the shout of the man who had just stepped out of the door behind him, and when the high bumper of the pickup hits, there is little pain, only a long, slow falling into darkness, a brief agony as the wheels pass over his sprawled body, and then nothing.

That's how it must have been. That's how. I heard a funny little moan. Mine. I wasn't in the dark lot with Wilmot, I was sitting at my own bright kitchen table with a newspaper full of toast crumbs spread out in front of me, fighting my other images, images of

Karen struggling with a silver-eyed madman, of Joey put out of a car and wandering onto a dark highway to be hit by a speeding pickup. I hugged myself and shivered. Staying cool for Mack, I thought, trying to jolly myself out of it.

No point in looking for a story about Chapin. He was no suicide. I set up the telephone answering machine and went to work. I suppose I could have stayed home, but my streak of cussedness was out to show R. Quentin Burns just how normal I could be.

Nobody was doing very much when I got there, late this time. The coffee-vending machine had a larger than usual gaggle of engineers clustered around it, and some of the eyes measured me as I came up the stairs and said good morning. Two violent deaths in one small group in the space of a week had left the rest of us suspicious and distant.

I was hoping Pedersen wouldn't be in, but he was sitting at his desk doing some calculations and nodded at me. As I hung up my coat, he turned and rested his hands on his thighs, his shaggy head cocked. "Have you heard anything?" he asked.

"In a way."

He looked alarmed. "It isn't good?"

"In a way." I sat down. "I got a call from Prunella Watson last night. Remember her?"

"The head of this peculiar organization that sends you out into the boondocks on various inconvenient occasions, yes."

"Yes. Somebody called her last Tuesday night, somebody who told her that a UFO had been seen in Roseville - not so - and got my name and phone numbers from her."

Pedersen sucked at his lip and nodded.

"I think I know who it was. The sighting she described was really one that happened a few years ago out in South Dakota, one that I worked on. Someone else was there. You remember the man at the airport, the one you decided to play a joke on?"

A half-second pause, and a stricken intake of breath. "He was doing something illegal?"

"I think so. Someone's stealing money from people who believe that giving their possessions away will help them go to UFO heaven, and I think it's the man at the airport. I think he was acting funny because he recognized me, and he wanted to see what I was doing."

Pedersen crumpled. "I never thought," he mumbled, after a moment. "He, then, is the one who has taken your family? Is he violent?"

"I don't know. I hope not. At least I don't

think he has anything to do with what happened to Chapin and Wilmot."

Pedersen stared past me at a corner of the floor, brow wrinkled and mouth slack. "I don't think you could forgive me this," he said. He sounded bleak. "I give you my word, I never intended harm. It was to have been only a joke, a mild revenge, because he behaved so oddly with regard to us. A teasing. But, of course, now we must find him. To find Karen. You will have to tell me all you can." His hands flopped. "That is, if you will trust me to help."

"Something just occurred to me," I said. "Somebody called me that night, Tuesday night." Good Lord, only a week ago? "I thought it was a wrong number, but now I wonder. It could have been Hawley checking to see who was home."

"You know his name?" Pedersen shouted. "That's wonderful! We can track him down now, certainly!"

"It may not be his real name," I pointed out.

"No matter. If he has used it long enough, he will have left traces." Pedersen scooted his chair over to the terminal and snatched up the phone. I shook my head. He'd done it again. I ought to be furious. I ought to be beating his fat head in. Instead, when he said. "The full name, please," I even spelled it for him.

Maybe I'd been wrong about him all the time: maybe the charm was just there, nothing he turned on. Or maybe it was just my own realism operating.

"Jamison!" Pedersen ripped off the sheet in the printer and shook it at me. "Look at this!"

Another time I'd have laughed at him, so indignant at having the tables turned: a nosy someone, at precisely 22:03:27 the night before – computers don't putz around about times – had tried to access Pedersen's working file, using his name and the group password. A password cagey Lars would, naturally, never dream of using as his own.

While he mulled that over, I used the phone to bring the hairy detective up to date, and got a scolding for waiting so long. Mack had already called him.

Pedersen started his search for Sergeant Hawley as soon as the phone was free, and I tried to list everything I could think of that might help. John Ferraro, for one: but Pedersen would have to get off the phone for that. I mentioned the possibility.

"Surely," he said, as if he hadn't heard

a word. "This Sergeant Hawley has no Minnesota driver's license."

Summer before last, when I had been embroiled in a different tangle, I'd grown used to such pronouncements.

"And no telephone, not even unlisted," Pedersen added.

"I told you it might not be his real name."

"Or, also possible, he might not live in Minnesota." Pedersen stared at the silent terminal for a moment. "Wait, I'll find out what flights were arriving and departing during the time we were in the airport."

"Arriving, Lars. He was too busy afterward to have left and come back."

"Arriving, then."

I went out to buy some coffee without even tossing for it. The intelligence of Western civilization runs on coffee, and my brain is no exception. The gaggle of engineers, composed of different individuals, still had the vending machine surrounded, and its production of colored fluid had become grudging. I went down to the cafeteria in search of another font of knowledge.

When I got back, Pedersen had a list of twenty-three arivals for the hour and a half before we had had our encounter with the silver-eyed man. Those eyes were his fortune, I suddenly realized: a fan loony enough might well think he was a UFOnaut in human guise, and be all the readier to part with his net worth in cash.

"Fast work," I said admiringly, looking over Pedersen's list.

"I called a travel agent," he admitted, downcast. "It seemed faster, if less intellectually challenging. Now, I'm afraid I'll have to call all these airlines to check their passenger lists, if they will do that for me. I think that also will be speedier, and speed is of the essence, now."

"In a few minutes, Lars. I want to try something else, first."

Pedersen's eyebrows jerked his forehead into lines as I extended one of the lidded Styrofoam cups, but he took it with a tentative smile and thanked me. "Please go ahead," he said.

John Ferraro wasn't home. I let the phone ring half of forever, until it began to sound like an echo down an infinite tunnel, and hung up feeling cheated.

"Start with the closest points of origin," I advised Pedersen, being an old hand at teaching my grandmother to suck eggs. "He can't be based too far away, if he's keeping tabs on a racket here."

"Bismarck, I guess, and Madison," he said, scanning the list. He hesitated before picking up the telephone. "Oh, I should say, I found yesterday evening that Leonard Fink's sixty-fifty birthday occurred on the seventh of the month."

"So he just retired?"

"It would seem so, yes." He sighed. "A disappointment."

"You can't win them all." Forty-five minutes later, we had lost another: none of the airlines had had a Sergeant Hawley on their passenger lists for any of the likely flights. Pedersen tried the single flight from L.A. out the sheer stubbornness, and gave up.

"Now, alas, after so much time on hold, I know how the computer feels with slow beings like us feeding data," he remarked.

I got hold of John Ferraro's wife just after lunch, and she promised to have him call me back. Then I called Mack, to see what, if anything, he'd learned about Sergeant Hawley, and got another scolding for taking so long to report to the Minneapolis police – they were working hand in hand, all right – and another lecture on minding my own business, as defined by Mackenzie Forrester.

"OK, OK," I said. "Have you got anything yet?"

"Give me a chance, J.J. I've got a lot of

hotels to check, and he might have a room anywhere, or be staying with a friend. This stuff is always slow, you know that."

I'd hung up before I realized that Mack already knew what Pedersen had just told me: no phone, no license. Well, at least he was working. "The police have computers now, don't they?" Pedersen asked, eyes narrowed.

"Forget it, Lars," I told him. "Mack will keep me posted. He's got nothing to tell me, or he wouldn't bother yelling at me."

The afternoon was enlivened by two gentlemen in plainclothes from Bill Chapin's precinct, who wanted to ask me just a few more questions – for example, would I account for every second of my time from Tuesday afternoon until early Friday morning, please?

Most of Tuesday was covered by work. Wednesday, during the day, was also – and Karen could have vouched for me for Wednesday night, except that I didn't know where Karen was.

The gentlemen found this very interesting. I showed them the hairy detective's card.

Twenty minutes of Wednesday evening and another twenty minutes on Thursday evening had been spent in the presumably unimpeachable company of one of their colleagues, said detective. "How come you came to work so early Thursday?" one of them demanded. I suggested that I had been upset. He suggested that I might have had to call someone for instructions.

I could have called from home a lot easier," I said.

"But then it would have been on your bill," the gentleman, whose philosophy, or maybe whose genes, dictated an unwavering gentle smile, observed. "Here, you could use the WATS line."

"And have it go right on the unit manager's list of numbers called, just in case he didn't know where to look for my contact."

Draw on that one. "In your statement the other day, you said that you failed to examine the body of Mr. Chapin when in his apartment."

"That's right. So what?"

In response to further questions I stated that I had seen two other gunshot victims and that was plenty for any lifetime, and it was his job to look the body over anyway. We parted with mutual dissatisfaction, and I restrained myself from raising a not-exactly-admonitory finger at R. Quentin Burns, who was hanging around smirking near the door of the conference room he had provided for the conversation.

"I am now suspected of murder as well as industrial espionage," I reported to Pedersen.

"Goodness, and you look so unremarkable," he responded. "Although I understand that's an advantage in such professions."

Nothing holds Pedersen down for long.

An hour later, he returned to the cubicle after a short absence with a late edition of the newspaper under his arm. "Look at this," he said.

A small item. The pickup truck that had hit Wilmot had been found, run into a small stand of spruce trees only a few hundred yards from the bar. It had been hotwired, and belonged to the car dealer next door to the bar. "A hundred engineers with specific knowledge of electrical circuits work across the road," Pedersen said. "Anyone could walk back to the plant in just a few minutes, and be on his way in his own car almost by the time the ambulance arrived."

"I guess so."

"What did you do, after you left Wilmot last night?"

"I went home and watched television."

"I was afraid of that." He regarded me

with his lips pinched together. "I think we have four crimes to solve now, yes? Quickly, before anyone else begins to think. I confess I am at a loss as to how to proceed."

"We could make a list," I said. "That's what Karen does, she makes lists."

"Karen solves –" He left the sentence unfinished. "Yes, that does seem an excellent idea," he added, in a hurry, and swung his chair toward the terminal.

The phone rang.

"Two-oh-three-nine, Jamison," I said into it.

"Hi, J.J., it's Jack Ferraro," said the caller. "What's this my wife is telling me about you needing some kind of help solving a crime? I thought you'd given that up."

"I would if I could," I assured him. "It's like this. Somebody called Prue Watson, remember her?" I collected a grunt from the other end of the line. "This guy used your name to get my name and phone number, as the person who investigates for CATCH in this area."

"You know that wasn't me, J.J.," Ferraro protested. "I already know you."

"I know. I said, *used* your name. What I think is that it was really this Sergeant Hawley I asked you about on Saturday."

"I told you then, I never heard of him."

"What about some of your crowd?"

"We don't even meet in the winter, J.J. Hardly anything happens, and when it does, like as not it turns out like this thing in North Dakota."

"I know. Listen. This guy, I'm pretty sure, has kidnapped my wife and son."

"Holy buckets." Ferraro always did have a strange way of talking. "The little guy, too? That's a shame, that really is. You want me to call around, see what I can find out?"

"I'd appreciate it, Jack. Whatever this guy is doing, he needed ten days to do it in. He told me that, said don't investigate for ten days. It's been seven. Soon, something's going to happen. What I'm guessing is that he's collecting a lot of money from people who think if they get rid of it they'll be taken for a ride in a UFO, and he wants to get the money and get out of the way. I don't want Karen and Joey lost in the scramble."

"One of those." Ferraro sounded thoughtful. "That's a little out of our line, J.J. I thought you knew."

It would be out of his line. Nobody nuts enough to fall for Hawley's line makes as much money out of a family business as John Ferraro has. "I know, believe me, but I thought you might have some, uh, less rational connections."

"Oh, boy, do I!" Ferraro paused. "Look, all I can think of to do is some calling around."

"Don't say who you're doing it for."

"You think I'm stupid?" he asked. "You'll be at this number?"

"Or home. I've got an answering machine set up there, so if I'm not either place, leave a message on it."

"A whole week they've been gone? And the bastard used my name?"

"That's what Prue said."

"And she'd make Abe Lincoln look like a mob leader," Ferraro sighed. "I'll get him for that. Taking a little kid, on my name! You got any idea what he looks like?"

"I'm not absolutely certain, but I think tall, skinny, dark hair, light gray eyes with a kind of shine to them, glasses."

"No bells. I'll get back to you as soon as I can," Ferraro promised, and hung up.

I went out to the john and got rid of some coffee residue. When I came back, Pedersen was busy at the terminal. I looked over his shoulder at what the printer was spewing forth.

Amluxen, J. C. read the top left-hand corner of each page. A lot of stuff I recognized as plain, honest work by Joyce Carol Amluxen. Nothing to show that she'd made any search of anyone else's files, or even attempted to.

B-u-r-n-s, Pedersen typed. I reached out and covered the transmit button with a hollowed hand. "That could get you in real trouble, Lars. Hit the one that tried to search your files, and I bet you dollars to dimes you'll find the password changed. Then what?"

Pedersen pulled at his long chin for a moment and touched the clear-entry key. "I'm not thinking ahead," he admitted. "I am too anxious to clear my name with you, Jamison." He sat back and stared at the keyboard for a moment. "I can get just as far if I can trick the central processor into telling me who has changed the password," he concluded. "I'll have to think about that, though."

I could have thought about it for a year and the central processor would never have heard from he. "I'm going home," I said. "Leave your chin alone, you'll make your beard grow in backwards."

Pedersen gave me a startled glance, but it was only reflex: the little gray cells were already turning into silicone chips, or trying to think that way.

"Don't work all night," I said, and left.

Chapter Ten

Pedersen called me at home that evening, the second time he had ever done so. "Any luck getting the central processor to spit out the passwords?" I asked.

"No." He sounded dispirited. In the background was a clamor of children's voices, some in English, some in Danish. "It is hard to tiptoe through your own garden without leaving footprints. I begin to recognize the limitations of my approach. Alas, I know no other. But I am glad to hear your voice, Jamison. I had feared you might have been arrested for one or another of these acts people seem to suspect you of performing."

I had a brief vision of myself as a tightrope artist, or a lion tamer, both occupations with less evident hazard than my own. "Not yet," I assured him. "But John Ferraro called me back. He's got somebody's address and a time tomorrow, Wednesday, night for these poor people to turn over their money. That's about all."

"It should be enough, surely?"

"No. He says the idea seems to be to get

all the money together and go somewhere to burn it." Pedersen made a sharp sound of pain. "He doesn't even know whether Hawley is going to be at the meeting, or whether he'll catch up with them later. I've been wondering what to do."

"Take them some money?"

"Aside from not having any, I can't just go knock on the door and ask to join in. A lot of these people know me."

"Surely, knowing your interest in flying saucers, they could be brought to believe that you, too . . ."

"Not a chance," I sighed. "That's just the problem. They know the kind of interest I take in UFOs – mostly debunking hoaxes and straightening out the mistakes. That's not at all what they're interested in. They need these extraterrestrials, somehow; they need to believe in them. A lot of them plain hate me for what I do."

"Even a madman may sometimes reason," Pedersen agreed. The clash of childish voices in the background reached a crescendo. "Excuse me," Pedersen murmured, and yelled something in Danish. The clamor stopped. I leaned against the doorframe looking into the family room, one stark slice of it lit by the kitchen light, as Pedersen delivered a brief, stiff lecture of which I understood only the word "no." Six kids, I thought. Karen and I had planned on two. When Pedersen came back on the line I could hardly talk. "Go on," he said.

I swallowed the lump in my throat. "I thought I might try following their caravan to wherever they're going to build their bonfire, but my car is such a light color.... I picked it to be visible, and I'm afraid one of them might spot it."

"The Volvo is dark green," Pedersen said.

"You'd lend me your car?" I was surprised. Like many fast and scatterbrained drivers, Pedersen didn't really trust anyone else to know how to handle a car.

"No. But I'd drive you."

"It could be dangerous, Lars," I warned him. "If their saucer doesn't show up, these people could blame it on us and get pretty nasty. Don't forget, they're giving up every single thing they own, just to get on the space ship."

"Jamison, I would be astonished if someone who has laid the careful plans this Sergeant Hawley seems to have would fail to take such a reaction into consideration. But how can they be planning to burn all? So large a fire?"

"Not really." I could hear the little voices rising again. "If they converted it all to cash, hundred-dollar bills, like the woman said –" I had to stop and explain about the woman who had gone to the St. Louis Park police.

"Why hundred-dollar bills? Why not thousand-dollar bills?"

"Because the government quit issuing anything bigger than hundreds, so that's all they can get. Big enough. You could still fit the net worth of six or seven ordinary people into a grocery bag and have plenty of room to fold down the top. A stack of hundreds an inch high is about twenty thousand dollars."

I could almost hear Pedersen deducting his mortgage from the market value of his house. "Perhaps many more people than seven," he said. Something crashed in the house that had given rise to this unsatisfactory subtraction. "Sven! Margritte!" Pedersen yelled.

"Lars," I managed to say. "It sounds as if you're needed there. I'll talk to you tomorrow, OK?"

"Yes, certainly," he said, and rang off. I slumped into one of the kitchen chairs, my chest still painfully squeezed, and one tear emerged from each eye and blazed a hot trail down each cheek. I wiped them away.

"Tomorrow," I whispered. "Tomorrow, Karen, tomorrow. I promise."

When I arrived at work the next morning, only two or three minutes early, Pedersen was already doing battle with the central processor.

"Any luck?"

"Not yet. Paranoid programmers," he said. "You'd almost think they worked for the Pentagon."

I didn't bother to remind him that some of them did. "Are you still willing to come with me tonight?" I asked.

"Oh, absolutely." Pedersen's lips pulled back over his teeth. "One needs to get out and about with others than one's family, don't you think?"

"If you say so." I hung up my coat and toed my galoshes off. "Any calls for me?"

"No. But then, I've been using the telephone."

I sat at my desk and contemplated my current problem. Should I tell Mack what I had learned from John Ferraro? This was his chance to arrest Hawley, get these people their money back. But would Hawley, under arrest, tell where Karen and Joey were being held? With him in jail, would they go hungry, thirsty, shut up somewhere in the dark and the cold?

Pedersen made an exasperated noise and slammed the phone back into its own cradle.

I picked it up and dialed Mack's home number.

"He's not here, J.J.," his wife said. "He's on duty."

"Oh." Not much chance of getting hold of him, then. "You don't know if he's made any progress in this UFO case, do you, Joy?"

"Last he mentioned it, he was trying to track down a customer at that print shop on Excelsior Boulevard. Some guy answering the description of this Hawley was in there last week, getting a lot of play money printed up. Hundred-dollar bills!" She laughed. "Mack said he must be planning to pass them in the dark, they're that bad."

"When was that, Joy?"

"Oh, Friday or Saturday. The print shop had kept some samples, I know that. They print in green one day a week, I forget which one."

"Not much help, is it?" I asked. "Thanks, Joy. Talk to you later."

"Wait! J.J., I want you to know, we're all hoping and praying for Karen and Joey. That they'll be home soon, unhurt."

"Thanks," I said, a little more softly.

I hung up deep in thought. So Mack had known, Friday or Saturday, that Hawley was planning to trade fake money for real, in some dark location. I'd split a six-pack with him Sunday afternoon, and he hadn't breathed so much as a hint. So much for keeping me posted. I glanced at Pedersen, scribbling hard on a pad of quadrille paper. I still couldn't quite bring myself to ask him to break into police records: what he thought of on his own I could talk myself into going along with, but for me to come right out and ask. . . .

I couldn't do it. But, on the other hand, if Mack was keeping secrets from me when it concerned my own wife and son, I didn't see any reason to spill everything I knew to him. And if I could get to Hawley, pacify him, plead with him, tell him he'd made a mistake, I wasn't on his trail at all, he might lead me to Karen. That night. Just under my collarbone, I felt a flutter as my heart skipped a few beats. Let him get his cash, then . . . just follow him. See where he went. Once he had his money, he couldn't want to keep my wife and kid, could he? Just follow him home and knock on the door. Quick, before he had a chance to do anything to them.

The printer began to chatter. Pedersen sat back and watched.

"You get through?"

"No. I changed projects." He folded his arms and continued to watch the paper roll up and out and stack neatly on the table behind the printer. "I should have done this a long time ago," he said.

I got up and looked over his shoulder. *Amluxen, J. C.* on the top of the page again, and then a bunch of things I recognized, in format at least: address, phone number, current salary, contributions to the United Fund, money going into the stock option plan, U.S. Bonds, medical and dental insurance for her kids, life insurance on herself.

"What's that going to tell you?"

"I thought that if I found someone who seems to provide inadequately for his future, in spite of the very generous fringe benefits offered to us, I might find someone with an outside source of income."

"I guess," I said doubtfully.

"Or contrariwise, if someone has sunk too much of his income into his future, he may have a motive for increasing his present cash flow."

"I guess," I said, still doubtful.

Burns, Robert Quentin, the printer clattered out. *Monthly base salary, $4,000; U.S. Bonds, $2.50*

"Not terribly patriotic, is he?" Pedersen commented. "It will take a couple of years to buy a bond at that rate."

Stock option, 6% base; United Fund, $75.00; retirement plan, 1%...

"He likes the company, anyway," I said. "He's in for the limit."

"All very dull," Pedersen agreed. "What else could one expect?"

Chapin, William Charles, the printer rattled onto the paper. *Deceased. Year-to-death earnings, pending supervisor's report.*

"Damn, they're fast," I said. "I guess they don't want to lay out an extra penny if they can help it."

Jamison, Joseph Richards.

"You can skip that one, Lars."

"Richards? With an s?"

"My mother's maiden name. I've been explaining it all my life." The printer's daisy wheel cheerfully trotted across the paper, rattling out all my private affairs.

"I'm glad to see that you have increased your rate of savings since the last time I had to do this, Jamison," Pedersen remarked.

The list took another four minutes to complete. Pedersen stared at it gloomily and added a request for Lisa, the secretary's, file. "I can't believe we have such a sensible set of coworkers," he exclaimed, paging through the folded paper. "Some moreso than others, of course, but no one out of line."

"Give it to me, we can study it later," I

said. I folded the printout in thirds and stuck it in the inside pocket of my overcoat. I had barely returned to my desk and picked up a pencil when one of the objects of our research stuck his head through our doorless door. "I thought I heard a printer going," he said. "You guys must spend the night here."

"Not a chance," Pedersen and I said in unison. The engineer leaned against the doorframe and we chatted for several minutes.

"You heard the latest on Mike Wilmot?" he asked. "He had four hundred bucks in his pocket when he was run down."

Pedersen shrugged. "Some people make a habit of carrying large amounts of currency."

"I sure don't. Do you, J.J.?"

"You've got to be kidding. Sometimes I have to borrow for lunch," I admitted. "But I don't know what Mike did."

"Well, all I can say, if that was one of his habits I'm sorry I ever bought him coffee." The engineer pushed off the doorframe and wandered away.

Pedersen turned back to the terminal. "Coffee?" I asked, suggestible as ever. At his nod, I went out to the vending machine without bothering with the ritual of tossing a coin. Hardly worth the effort. I was back at my desk trying to warm my cold fingers in the steam from the cup when Pedersen announced that Wilmot's bank account had shown no unusual activity. He'd drawn a hundred and fifty in cash when he deposited his last paycheck, and that was it.

"Interesting," Pedersen said. "Can someone have paid for his silence?"

For his silence? Or for finding out what I knew about Bill Chapin's death? In that case, I'd left something out of my little scenario, the report to the person so anxious to know... but the bartender hadn't mentioned anyone, had said specifically that Wilmot was alone at the bar....

I glanced at my left wrist. Texas Instruments told me it was 8:38. Ten and a half more hours, and I'd be sitting outside a house on the western fringe of Minneapolis, waiting to see what Sergeant Hawley did. The thought made my belly cramp.

John Ferraro called again, about mid-afternoon. "I've got a little more for you, J.J.," he said. "Not much. It seems that these people are expecting the UFO to pick them up on Friday night at the same place they're going to burn their money. Only I don't know where that is, yet – I don't think they do, either. Each of them has fifty dollars to last them those two days. Generous, huh?"

"Wowee," I said. "Say, Jack, something's been bothering me. If they're all selling their cars, how are they going to drive anywhere?"

"Borrow or rent, I guess. I do know the stuff really is being sold – I was tempted to pick up a nice Toyota, cheap, but I dunno. I wouldn't feel good driving it. Too much like taking candy from a baby, you know? And I found out something else. This has been going on a long time, J.J. Since last fall, at least. Some of these guys listed their houses with this agent that promises a sale in three months, or he'll buy the house himself, way last October."

"He buys? I hadn't heard about that."

"You don't watch enough late-night television. It's been a real blitz, like that guy who used to want to dry out your basement. I hear a few have already sold. The guy I talked to has his closing set for Friday, that's how I found out the transport would be delayed, and he's signed his arms and legs away on a loan from a finance company to get in on the cash burning, you know?"

Holy buckets, as Ferraro might have said. "Thanks, Jack."

"You know what makes me mad? All these jokers are real old people, all their friends or relatives died or moved away, they're scared in their houses because of all the crime, and then this guy comes along and takes everything they worked all their lives to get. Want company?"

"I think I can handle it. Thanks."

"Good luck, J.J. You catch that guy that used my name, you knock his teeth in for me, OK?"

"I think I'll just ask him where my family is, if it's all the same to you, Jack."

"Just like my business. If you want something done right, you got to do it yourself. Take care, J.J."

I promised to take care and hung up. Pedersen was gazing at me, his long face even longer than usual. "You were right about Hawley," I said. "He's got himself an out for the saucer not showing up."

He nodded. "We will have dinner together, yes? I've arranged with my wife. I would invite you to the house, but it is a long drive and we might not have time."

"I'd invite you to mine," I said, "but we might not have food."

"There is a Chinese restaurant quite close to you, is there not? We can solve that problem with their able assistance."

"Whose computer did you find that listed in?"

"No one's." Pedersen slumped, a picture worth a thousand words of dejection. "I looked it up in the Yellow Pages."

He'll live like the rest of us yet.

Coffee-scented smoke hung in the air as we got out of the Volvo and clambered over the mounded snow onto the sidewalk near the restaurant. Pedersen sniffed appreciatively.

"Fire in their roaster," I explained. Not the first, either, but then the shop that sold the fancy coffees and teas had prudently located almost in the lap of the fire station. The Chinese restaurant was jammed into a sliver of storefront right next door.

"Ah, an *ex*cellent Chinese tea," Pedersen exclaimed, as he sipped at the cup the waiter filled for him. "A good omen."

"Get Lipton's in a place like this and you're in deep trouble," I agreed.

"Cuisines of Szechwan," Pedersen read from the menu. He grinned. "Those are the ones that bore one's frontal sinuses out, are they not? I am treating, Jamison, I feel it only right. Please do not read the prices."

The prices were nothing extravagant, anyway, and suddenly I had an appetite. I made no murmur as Pedersen ordered wonton soup, egg rolls, Mandarin chicken and shrimp with lobster sauce, and moo goo gai pan, although the waiter's eyebrows lifted slightly. It said right there on the menu that they didn't stint on quantity, and they didn't.

"The only trouble with Chinese restaurants is that they give one no butter," Pedersen said, pouring more tea. The idea of buttered egg rolls left me slightly queasy, but the queasiness vanished when the soup was set in front of me.

Several times during the meal I caught myself just shoveling the food in, anxious to get to the house where the loonies - er, fans - were meeting well ahead of time. A crime to treat good food that way, I thought, and then I wondered what Karen had eaten, what Joey had been fed, and my appetite vanished with my fork halfway between the plate and my mouth. I picked at what I had left in front of me while Pedersen savored every grain of rice he had on his plate and arranged for the leftovers to be packed up.

He looked at what I had left and pursed his lips. "It is a crazy hope we have, isn't it, Jamison?"

"I know it."

"We'd best go, however." We pulled out of the parking spot at only ten past six: darkness had already fallen, but we would still be in position to observe the house in good time.

Five minutes later, we turned out of the ruts worn in the snow of a well-traveled road into a smaller, still slush-clogged street near the western edge of the city. At Pedersen's suggestion, we drove past it once. Lights were on in the two front rooms, a living room and a bedroom to judge by the walls, a boring beige in the first and blue paper with huge rosebuds in the second. "It looks empty," Pedersen said.

It did. No curtains, no furniture, just the overhead lights on. As we passed the house and I looked back, I saw someone walk into the bedroom, too slight a glimpse to hope to recognize.

Pedersen circled the block once more, choosing his parking place. He tucked the Volvo into a space on the opposite side of the street from the house, a couple of houses down and with a driveway right behind us. "We can't get parked in, now," he explained. "And if we must turn around, we may perform our reversal in the driveway."

I slid far down in the seat, not wanting any of the arriving loonies to recognize me. Pedersen pulled a dark wool cap over his fair hair and also slumped down, not quite so far. "No one has come yet," he whispered.

"We're half an hour early."

"Do I dare play the radio very softly?"

"Sure, why not?"

Pedersen turned the radio on, very low, so that I couldn't quite make out the words the newscaster was reading. Pedersen, as he has told me more times than I can count, has excellent hearing.

Two people came along the sidewalk from behind us and strolled on past without seeming to take any notice of two men in a parked car. So far, so good, but even with that boost to my confidence, I shifted in the seat, uncomfortable already.

"I read a book, not long ago," Pedersen whispered. "About a private investigator. He maintained that this is the worst part of such an occupation, waiting in a parked car for something to happen."

"Like what?"

"Oh, in his case, for the wrong man to come out of a front door. Or for a man to come out of the wrong front door." I couldn't see much difference between the cases, myself. Maybe it depended on who did the hiring.

A woman jogged past with a large dog on a long leash. For a moment, the dog threatened to take more than a passing interest in the Volvo, but the woman cursed and tugged at the leash until the beast had favored Pedersen's front tire with a squirt and loped on ahead of her, dragging her arm out straight. As she stumbled under the streetlight, still shouting at the dog, I saw that she had striped her jogging suit with reflective tape. A good idea.

I hadn't jogged since before I left for North Dakota, I remembered. I should at least have dusted the rebounder; Karen would be nagging at me about my lack of exercise.

Another car drove slowly past us and pulled in toward the curb down the block, past the house we were watching. The headlights died. I watched. Nothing. "Did anyone get out of that car, Lars?" I asked.

"What car?"

I reminded myself that I was not working with a professional private eye, but only with a man who had read about one. All I could do was hope that something had blocked my view, that some unconcerned homeowner had emerged from the vehicle and trotted up his front walk without my seeing him. You're just antsy, J.J., I told myself.

Still, I hadn't taken my eyes off that car. I hadn't seen a dome light come on. And was that the brief flare of a cigarette being lighted, or a trick of my straining eyes?

I scrunched down even lower. My hands were so cold, they were beginning to hurt, although the car was still reasonably warm. I took off my gloves and blew on my fingers. Nerves.

"I'm going to walk around the block," Pedersen announced. He had slipped out of the car before I could protest, but at least he closed the door quietly and turned back, to walk away from that other car, the one in which Sergeant Hawley was perhaps waiting to see if the house had been staked out. I turned the radio up a fraction and listened to a special report on confrontations between Israeli soldiers and U.S. Marines on a peace-keeping mission in Lebanon. Lebanon seemed infinitely far away, something on another planet. My own planet had shrunk to this small dark world in which I waited, the point of light from the radio the only intrusion from outside.

Pedersen almost gave me a heart attack, opening the driver's-side door and sliding in. He turned the radio down. "Two people are in the house," he said. "I watched from the alley. Neither is the man we saw at the airport. One is a short and very plump woman of perhaps fifty years with oddly yellow hair."

"She's the one who owns – used to own – the house."

"You know her?"

"I've seen her a few times. I looked her up in my files last night, when Ferraro gave me the address. They had a group that met in another house they lived in once, bunch of nuts, invited me to speak to them one night a few years ago. Disaster."

"Ah, I see. She is going from room to room, perhaps saying good-bye to the house. But what have they done with their furniture?"

"Sold it, most likely. Who's the other person?"

"A man of the same age, taller and darker but also fat."

"Her husband."

"No one has come to this meeting, then," Pedersen said. He sounded anxious. "Might it have been called off? Because someone has discovered that this Ferraro has given you the information?"

The Volvo had about five thousand dials, but no clock. I pushed the button to light up my watch. "It's still twenty minutes early," I pointed out. "No reason to get nervous."

"I see now why these night-long watches become tedious," Pedersen remarked. Lights of a car coming the opposite way reflected off the packed snow into his face. He dipped his head so that the dark watch cap took the light.

The car pulled over to the other side, which was empty because of the one-side parking ban the last snow had brought us. After a short wait one person got out and went up to the house and rang the doorbell. A minute later the door opened; the light spilling out showed an elderly man, carrying nothing in his hands but wearing an overcoat with a bulging pocket. He went in, and the door cut the light off, leaving only the lighted doorbell button as a tiny beacon for fools, shining through the night.

"Shall I go see what is happening?" Pedersen whispered.

"No."

"You are not curious?"

I didn't point out that his curiosity, back in the airport, was what had brought us here. "I'm curious as hell," I said, "but I don't want anyone to notice us."

"Oh." Pedersen let himself slip down in the seat again. "One old man isn't going to bring Hawley much money."

"We don't know that. That house over there probably sold for eighty thousand dollars. Depending on the mortgage, they could have cleared quite a bit."

Ten more minutes went by, during which National Public Radio kept us informed and Pedersen groused, in a whisper, continually.

A second car pulled up on the other side of the street. Two people got out, a short, dumpy woman gesturing at a man who moved stiffly toward the house we were watching. The woman pulled at his arm, under which he clutched a small bag. He struck backward with his elbow and gained the steps, made a lunge for the doorbell. The door was opened by the fat man, and in the light of the opening door I saw the newcomers were an elderly man and a middle-aged woman. The woman grabbed the former homeowner by the front of his sweater. He gave her a small shove as the old man slipped into the house and, as she staggered back a step, slammed the door in her face. She climbed through a row of junipers to the living room window and pounded on it, then changing her mind, hurried back to her car and took off in a shower of sloppy snow.

"Going for the police?" Pedersen whispered.

Quite possibly. But she was heading toward St. Louis Park, and the house was in Minneapolis. Sure to delay things somewhat, even with the new county-wide emergency system.

Several more arrivals in the next couple of minutes: I counted ten. Two parked – I guess you don't worry about $25 parking tickets when you are about to be swept off to a better world – some were dropped off, and one came in a cab. Then a yellow fastback pulled up to the curb and Sergeant Hawley got out.

Pedersen hissed. "That's him," I agreed. "Don't move."

Hawley looked around slowly, pausing to glance at each of the cars parked along the street. I wondered how bright the little light of the Volvo's radio might be, to eyes accustomed to the dark. Not too bright: Hawley sauntered up to the house and pushed the doorbell. The door opened and he was welcomed inside.

"Shall I go look through a window?" Pedersen whispered.

"No. Someone might come late, or they might decide to leave right away. If anyone spots you, there'll be hell to pay."

Pedersen settled back, giving the impression of a hen with slightly ruffled feathers. Through the bare windows of the house, I could see Hawley gesturing. Then, one by one, the people there disappeared from the lighted front room for a moment and returned. The light in the bedroom went out. People began buttoning coats, and the group emerged all at once from the front door. The light in the living room went out. The husband came out and pulled the door shut. The group stood talking on the sidewalk for a moment or two, and then Hawley and three others started for the yellow car. Hawley stopped and said something. Two of the three turned back, the one remaining got into the car with Hawley, and when the others had distributed themselves among the three remaining cars, the procession slowly got underway.

Hawley first. "Wait until they get past before you start the engine," I said. Pedersen grunted.

The other cars got into line. "We're headed in the wrong direction, of course," Pedersen said. "It's been that sort of week." He put the car into reverse and backed into the driveway. "Which way are they going?"

"Left."

Pedersen pulled out of the driveway, switched on his lights, and turned left at the next intersection. The tail lights receded ahead of us.

"Wait, they're going around the block," I said, as the lead car slowly turned left again. "Damn, are they just turning, or are they checking to see if they're followed?"

"Checking for followers," Pedersen said, with conviction. "It's what I would do myself." He made a quick right turn and then another, skidding into and out of the ruts worn in the soft snow, and speeded to the end of the block, where he slid to a stop while I clenched my fists and prayed.

"Yes, here they come." The four cars, one after another, crossed the intersection to our right and came toward us. As they passed, Pedersen swung into line behind them. "I hope they don't notice if I stay with them too long," he worried aloud. "If I could only disguise the car!"

"Let's hope they're thinking of something else."

Pedersen laughed. "In their place, I'd be thinking of my millimeter of hundred dollar bills."

The string of cars gained France Avenue, the western boundary of the city of Minneapolis, and turned south. Pedersen followed fairly closely: traffic on France wasn't heavy, but it was steady, and too long a wait to take the turn would have lost us our quarry. At 50th Street we all turned right, Pedersen and I through the tail end of the amber light. "I hope they don't do that too often," I said. "This is no time to get stopped for running a light."

"Fear not. I have not had a ticket in my life."

With his luck, he was probably telling the truth. The yellow car in the lead lollygagged along 50th Street, through the Edina business district, and speeded up only slightly when it had passed the bluish lights of the supermarket parking lot that appeared on our left. "They have good cheese in there," Pedersen remarked. "I got some excellent *getöst* just a couple of weeks ago." He slowed to let someone run across the street in front of the library.

"I'm glad you've got such good manners," I said. "But let's not lose our boy." I leaned far to the right to see if I could pick up any turn signals. "I guess he's not taking 100," I said.

"On the contrary, he has just signaled his left turn," Pedersen corrected, pushing his own turn-signal lever up. We made the turn well behind the convoy. Someone passed us on the approach ramp, splattering dirty water on the windshield. Pedersen turned on the wipers and got a smear of mud for his efforts. He cursed, in Danish.

As we loafed along behind the newcomer, a fine snow began to fall, just enough to wet the road and windshield and become a mist in the headlights. I sighed. Mild as this winter had been, other than one whopper of a storm in the week before New Year's Day, we'd been building our snowcover every other day a quarter inch at a time. I was sick of it. On the other hand, this time it did help clear the windshield.

"Shouldn't you close up a bit?" I asked nervously. "I can't see the tail lights very well, with all this slop."

"Fear not," Pedersen said again. Swinging into the passing lane, he accelerated steadily until he had passed the yellow car, then settled back in front of it.

"What are you doing? What if he turns off?"

"Relax, Jamison. Have I not just told you that I had read a book about a private detective? I know all about this. The next exit he can take is to the Crosstown. We will pretend to use it, and if he does also, we will keep going. Otherwise we will let them all get past, and return to the road."

This maneuver was seconds away: I braced myself. Pedersen signaled his right turn, slowed, and pulled into the deceleration lane. The yellow car went straight. Pedersen cut his turn signal, rode along the snow-narrowed shoulder, and pulled back into the procession behind the car that had passed us getting onto the highway. "There, you see?" he said. "Piece of pie."

The snow thickened as we continued

south, and Pedersen's mouth took on a firm, tight set. "Bad driving," he said once. Past the junction with the Interstate, Highway 100 turns into something called Normandale Boulevard, and the surface there was slicker, for some reason I couldn't see. I think even Pedersen was relieved when the speed limit dropped, but we weren't quite prepared for the skid the car ahead of us took: first sideways onto the edge of the shoulder, then, as the driver fought for control, sideways in the other direction into the passing lane. Pedersen hissed, and my fingers cramped onto the edges of my seat. The lights slued wildly as the little sedan came halfway around again, and wound up going more or less in the direction of travel with the rear end sashaying for another fifty yards.

My heart pounding, I glanced at Pedersen. His knuckles stood out in his fists, clamped on the wheel; his jaw muscles corded his cheeks, but the Volvo held the road and came out somehow ahead of the car that had skidded. I glanced back into it and glimpsed a pale, slack-mouthed face that looked something like Mack Forrester's, with his big mustache.

"Waltz me around again, Rosie," I said. Pedersen didn't reply.

The road narrowed a bit and Pedersen

dropped back from the end of the procession a few more car lengths. "I think they must be going to Hyland Lake," he said. "What do you think?"

"We passed the turnoff onto Eighty-fourth Street already," I pointed out.

"There's another way in," Pedersen reminded me. "Across Old Shakopee Road and up 28 to – what is it? – Bush Lake Road. They could be going 'round about, to discover followers."

"Could be." Hyland Lake Park Reserve wasn't perfect, but it would be a reasonable place for Hawley to choose: the cross-country skiers would have been shooed out at sunset, and the park would be empty at this time of a winter day. The picnic area at the north end of the lake was furnished with grills in which the prospective UFOnauts could broil their earthly goods to their hearts' content, and parts of the reserve were open country where a UFO could land – or, given the surely superior extraterrestrial technology, it could land on the ice of the lake, even this winter.

Right. Pedersen hung back and put his fog lamps on as the caravan turned off onto Old Shakopee Road. "It will look like an entirely different car, now," he explained as he made the turn after them. "I hope." The snow had let up a little; I began to hope that it was just a longish flurry, and that we wouldn't find ourselves trapped when it came time to leave.

Hawley had hit what might have been an unexpected impediment: a chain had been stretched across the access road between the entrance shack and a sturdy post set on the other side of the drive. Other sturdy posts had been placed to discourage driving around the end of the chain, and whoever had plowed the road had shoved up some big piles of snow to reinforce the idea. Pedersen and I drove on around the next curve and stopped.

"Now what?"

"Now we wait,""" Pedersen said. "In a few minutes we will turn around and drive back and see what he has managed to do. I will be quite surprised if this Sergeant Hawley has not brought bolt cutters."

"He may not be as bright as you are, Lars."

"That much money could make a congenital idiot incandesce." Pedersen leaned against the wheel, forearms crossed, the lights turned down to parking lamps. "It's a warm night," he said. "I'm glad for all those old men, who should be tucked up at home and not braving a January evening."

"If they still had homes."

"True," he sighed. He turned on the headlights as he spoke, and made a careful K turn in the road, several passes to avoid the treacherous edges. I thanked my lucky stars he'd come along with his tight-turning Volvo. I wouldn't want to try the same turn in my own barge. "Now," Pedersen said, and shut off the lights.

We coasted back with just the fog lights, straining to see what was going on at the chain. Pedersen hissed and cut off even the fog lights: the last car was just crossing the cut chain. "Stronger than I thought, or his cutters were inadequate," he said. "I don't like men who make mistakes, not on occasions like this." He had killed the engine with the lights; now he let the car drift into the widened part of the crossroad formed by the turnoff to the park and stopped. "Do we risk a flashlight?" he asked.

"Only to save our necks."

"I'll bring it along, then. In the glove compartment, please, Jamison." I handed him the flashlight and we got out and leaned the doors shut, two loud, loud clicks in the snowy night. The sky was gray-pink above us, much lighter than it had looked from inside the car, indistinguishable from the snow where the nearest bare hill formed the horizon. "Not too dark," Pedersen observed.

"Once our eyes finish adjusting, we should be able to see quite well."

He started along the plowed access road, walking in the tracks of the cars that had just passed. My galoshes chink-chinked with each step. I wanted to take them off, but underneath I had only the thin-soled dress shoes I'd worn to work and I sure didn't want to add frostbite to my other worries. One of which, I realized, was that clothes suitable for concealment in the dark interior of a parked car weren't so great a disguise against snow, not even at night. I looked back and saw the Volvo hulking black against the white snowbank, shorn of its background of dark highway and the invisibility of belonging.

"Lars," I whispered, wanting to go back and wait around the bend for the caravan to leave. He shushed me with a backward shake of his hand and I followed, feeling helpless and exposed.

The cars were lined up side by each in the parking lot, dark. No one around. Pedersen picked the nearest one, a blue or black or dark gray sedan, and crouched against it, scanning the hill. It looked like a good idea: I hunkered next to him and looked up.

"There," I whispered, pointing to a reddish flash of light through the trees. Not flame, a flashlight with a red surround. Pedersen pointed toward a dark thicket of some leafless shrubs, and we made for that. It would cover us for only a few yards, but as if to make up for that, a ski trail had been groomed next to it. Pedersen stopped suddenly, glanced again at the hillside above us, and knelt to flash his light at the ground. Fresh footprints pocked the snow.

I glanced behind us and saw lights on the road that crossed the reserve. "Somebody coming," I whispered.

Pedersen looked. "Possibly." He returned his attention to the hillside where we had seen the flashlight. A small point of orange glow could be seen now, the source over the crest of the hill. He sighed softly and struck out for the light, choosing his route to avoid the drifts remaining from the late-December storm. Slick walking, all the same, and several times I slipped. The buckles on my galoshes sounded like Big Ben chiming to me, but there were no sounds of alarm ahead of us. Just as I was about to be able to see over the crest of the hill, Pedersen stopped so short I collided with him and almost went down again. "Listen," he breathed in my ear.

I could hear voices ahead of me, one complaining about the fire, which wasn't going well enough to be sure the money would burn, another wondering aloud if it would be safe to spray more charcoal lighter on what was already burning. A third, remarkably sensible, answered with a sharp, "No!" Hawley, probably.

None of this was what had caught Pedersen's ear: he had turned and was looking down toward the parking lot, and now I saw what he had heard, two cars coming through the illegally opened gate and up the drive toward the lot. No lights going, not even headlights, but the glass lumps on the car roofs stood out distinctly against the pinkish hue of the snow. Four dark-clothed figures wearing what looked like riding breeches got out of the cars and scanned the slope. I saw an arm lift and point toward the light.

"Lars, get moving, we've got to get to Hawley, get him to tell us where he's got Karen and Joey, before these guys arrest this whole gang for trespassing."

"And you and me." Lars hurried through the sloppy snow, not at all careful about noise now. I could hear faster footsteps squishing up the hill.

The scent of kerosene caught at my nostrils. As we came over the crest of the hill, I saw the old, yellow-lighted faces lift to stare at us, their gloved hands coming up protectively, Hawley's eyes glittering at me across the charcoal grill, which had just blazed up. Black, leaflike forms rose into the night with small sparks falling from them.

"Look at that money," shouted a deep voice behind us. "Look at that money. It's all fake. You've been tricked."

The tableau stayed frozen for a heartbeat or two. Hawley clutched the top of a grocery bag closed and took a step backward. Someone snatched at the bag and it tore, bundles of money spilling onto the snow. One of the old men leaned down and picked one of the bundles up. "It is fake," he quavered. "This isn't what we gave him. It's play money."

A low growl began in the crowd, and someone snatched my arm from behind and twisted it upward behind me. "Police," he boomed in my ear. Hawley turned and floundered down the long snowy incline toward the lake, chased by two of his victims.

"Get him, get him," I shouted. "Don't let him get away, he's got my wife and son!"

Hawley stumbled through a low drift and dropped onto the windswept frozen lake. He recovered his balance and started to run across the slushy, treacherous surface. In any other January, he might have been across the white ice and into the trees on the other side of the lake and away, but this year the weather had been much too mild, the snow cover erratic; his feet slipped and he fell to his knees on the puddled surface with a splash.

One of the men pursuing him eased onto the ice, ran to catch up and tackled Hawley just as he got to his feet. Again he splashed down, full length this time, and the pursuer grabbed his head and smashed it into the ice, his high angry voice slowing to keep time with the deadly rhythm. "My whole life," he shrieked, the words thin on the water-scented air. "My whole life!"

The cop holding me let go and plunged through the snow toward the lake. "Don't hurt him, don't hurt him," I yelled, "don't hurt him, I need him," running through calf-deep snow in what felt like slow motion, gasping for breath.

Hawley stopped struggling. The old man smacked his head into the ice twice more. A shot. The old man got up and ran for shore, slipping and scurrying on hands and knees to reach for the outstretched hand of the cop: not a shot. Ice breaking. The cop heaved, and the man scrambled up the bank. Hawley lay still.

I had almost reached the lake, my jacket and overcoat abandoned in the snow somewhere behind me. The cop glanced at me and turned back toward the lake, where a wide gray stain on the snow showed that the ice had thinned.

"Get back, get back," somebody yelled. "Can't you see the thin spot? You'll go in!"

"Yeah, let him drown," added the plump blonde.

The corniced snow of the bank crumbled under me and I landed hard on my butt. "Hey!" the cop exclaimed.

I launched myself onto the ice, scrabbling across the shaking surface, intent on the still body less than ten yards away. "Damn it, you," I said through my teeth. "You can't die on me, not yet." Pedersen shouted my name.

A small depression had appeared in the ice under Hawley's legs and was filling with black water, but his head and chest still rested on sound ice. The lake snapped again. As it quivered I threw myself flat on the wet, quaking surface and wormed toward Hawley, gasping at the cold. My stomach cramped around the moo goo gai pan, but I got a grip on some part of Hawley's clothes and dragged backward. His head dragged through the water, but I couldn't be bothered about it then; my arms and legs were already numbing and I could only scuttle crabwise for shore, cursing my water-filled galoshes. I gained the edge of the ice and boosted my burden toward the orange light that was the only thing I could see.

Hands grabbed and Hawley lightened and I fell to my knees. Someone splashed beside me; I was shoved and hauled onto the snowbank that overhung the shore, a slap of grainy ice into my face. I noticed that I was shivering. My fingers had quit working. "Move, move," one of the cops said, pulling at me, and someone reached past me to help another man onto the bank.

"Jamison, Jamison, are you all right?" Pedersen yanked at my shirt; he got it off and hung my dry jacket and coat over my shoulders, but I couldn't thank him. My teeth chattered so hard I was afraid I would bite my tongue, and my stomach was still intent on ridding itself of foreign influences.

"Come on, fella, come on," one of the cops urged. "We got to get you warmed up, quick." I thought longingly of the survival kit in my Ford, parked in my driveway ten impossible miles away.

"Is he dead?" Pedersen asked the cop bent over Hawley.

"I can't tell yet."

"Who cares?" asked the plump blonde.

"I do," I tried to say, but all that came out was a croaked, "Ah-ah-ah-ah –"

Pedersen took over. "This man has kidnapped Mr. Jamison's wife and small son," he said, the words clipped and urgent. "We want to ask him where they are being held."

The cop bending over Hawley looked up. "Well, you may get your chance, but it won't be soon."

My shivering had settled down to a steady rhythm, and the convulsions in my belly had eased up slightly. I still couldn't talk. "Get him down to one of the cars," somebody said, and I found myself hustled along, down the path to the parking lot, the water in my boots sucking at my feet. That surprised me. I thought it had frozen.

The cop dumped me into the back of a squad car and reached into the front and turned the heater on high. "You Jamison?" he asked.

I nodded, enough to distinguish it from the shivers, I hoped.

"Who's the Swede?"

"P-p-p-p –"

"Forget it, we'll catch it later." He slid into the front seat and closed the door and keyed his microphone all in one fluid motion, and said something into his radio, three incomprehensible sentences half-composed of numbers. Then he turned on his spotlight and scanned the other cars in the lot. He started punching license numbers into a small computer console that sat on the differential hump, up under the dash: something familiar, something I could understand, that comforted me somehow, even hunched frozen in the back seat with my face against the screen between the seats.

"Well, what do you know?" the cop said. "Every one of them rented."

"Hawley," I got out. The word set off a new round of shivers. Oh, Karen, I really blew it, I thought.

"Who, the guy on the lake?"

I nodded. "Money from others," I squeezed out, nipping my tongue between my teeth in the middle of the last word. "Back seat of yellow car."

It had to be there. That was the only place he could have made the switch, by throwing the bag of hundred-dollar bills he had collected into the back seat, and then just casually taking out the bag of fake money he'd stashed there earlier. All under the less-than-watchful eye of one of his victims. That was another question: how had he talked them out of having three ride along?

The cop got out of the car and shut the door. The heater hummed away, but the blast of cold air that came in as the door opened and shut, the same air that had seemed so balmy for the past week or more, started me shivering hard again. Up the hill, the faint glow of the money fire had gone out. A flashlight came down the hillside, flickering behind the shrubs Pedersen and I had used as cover only minutes before. Far away, at the fringe of my hearing, a siren yawped at the pink night.

I managed to unclamp my arms from my sides and get them into my sleeves and turn the lapels of my jacket and coat up, although my teeth were still chattering so hard I was afraid they might shatter. The flashlight I had been watching abruptly shone clear at the near end of the shrubs, swaying from side to side in the hand of one of the policemen. Behind him came a tall cop, paired with Pedersen, the two of them lugging Hawley in a three-hand carry. Hawley's head rolled lightly on the cop's shoulder; a moment later the spotlight of the second squad car was trained on the lower part of the hill. Long black shadows sprang alive, weaving over the faces of the twelve postulants to the Order of UFO as they picked their way down the hill, one at a time, heads down, whether with disillusionment and shame or a desire not to trip, I didn't know. Another cop brought up the rear. When the procession got to the plowed-out lot, they fanned out to the cars and the cop came along and let them in, hanging onto the keys. The plump blonde seemed to be crying into a wad of tissues. I wondered if she had had special permission from Hawley the High Priest to keep a personal box of Kleenex.

Pedersen and the man with him had done something with Hawley while I watched the others, and now the first cop down the hill was talking to them in the shadows near the other squad car. Four cops, I counted now. The one that went down on the lake to help Hawley and me must have been made of steel.

The cop whose car I was sitting in came up to the little group next to the car. I saw Pedersen's head snap up, and he, too, had something to say: his hands spread wide. I wished I had his hearing.

The conference continued for a minute or two, and then the first cop walked back to the car I was sitting in and stuck his head in at me. "Think you could stand to get out for a minute?" he asked. "I've got something over here your friends seem to think you'd be interested in."

I clenched my jaw as well as I could and got out of the car and followed the sadist over to the yellow fastback. The shiver came back with a vengeance.

"There's a kid in here," the cop said, throwing open the driver's side door. The dome light came on. Lying on the back seat, wrapped closely in a plaid wool blanket and sound asleep, was Joey.

Chapter Eleven

But my joy soon froze. . . .

Joey, in the back of the ambulance, looked like a kid in the ordinary deep sleep of early childhood but I couldn't rouse him. He flopped as slack-jointed as the broken chain we had driven across when I shook him, took one deep breath, and settled back to his light, ordinary, small-child-dreaming breathing.

"Doped," said the paramedic, a kid who looked young enough himself to be in high school. "Probably wanted to keep him quiet."

Another chill shook me, and the kid – in the dim light I couldn't tell if he was Indian or half-Asian – glanced at me, a worried glance. He pushed his straight black hair out of his eyes and looked out the back of the ambulance at the scenery dropping behind us. The other ambulance went shrieking past us on the turn into Normandale Boulevard, carrying Hawley and the chilled cop.

"Did you see the guy whose head got banged?" I asked.

The kid brushed his hair out of his eyes again and nodded.

"How did he look to you?"

"Not good."

I twisted around to look out the front window of the ambulance, which was cruising at a sedate twenty or twenty-five miles an hour along the way Pedersen and I had come, maybe half an hour before. The driver's arms looked stiff against the wheel. The wipers skimmed lazily over the windshield, pushing fine lines of wet snow across it to pack into a small bank that had formed at the limit of their arc. Not much traffic: just the monochrome streetlamps, the occasional traffic light, the lights along the side of the road looking lost and useless, and the night again black and ominous through the glass. I wondered how Pedersen was doing.

"You think he'll be able to talk by morning?" I asked.

"Your kid?"

"No, that other guy."

"There's always miracles," the paramedic said, after a pause.

Joey took another deep, sighing breath. The kid glanced at him, a professional, give-away-nothing glance. I wondered if the way Joey was breathing was a good sign, or a bad one, but even with my fingers twisted together as tight as they'd go and my jaw muscles knotted, I couldn't get up the guts to ask. I thought of Hawley, bundled so carefully out of the back of the squad car onto a stretcher. His breathing had been harsh and irregular: just the way the paramedics moved, anybody could tell he was in trouble. "Oh, Karen," I sighed. The kid glanced at me, his face impassive or inscrutable as the case might be, and out the back of the ambulance.

I had a blanket over me, a gray wool blanket that held in some warmth, but underneath it my pants were still wet and clinging to my legs. I kept shifting and picking at the cloth. As I moved my feet, my shoes squelched inside the galoshes – the kid had advised against taking them off – and I wondered if the shoes, $85 Florsheims, would ever be the same again. Instantly I was ashamed to be thinking of things like that at a time like that, even if they were my best pair.

I know the ambulance ride can't have taken the hours it seemed: it was only a little over six miles long altogether. Probably twenty minutes at the outside. After the dim, leisurely ride that seemed to take so long, and that left me lulled and lethargic, the bright light and bustle of the emergency room stunned me.

Joey was the one that got the attention. Another kid, maybe twenty, unwrapped the plaid blanket and I saw with a shock that Joey was wearing his own fuzzy blue sleepers with the crossed bats and baseball embroidered over his heart. He sighed again as he was lifted onto a gurney and rolled away, a limp little bundle. Somebody in white came around with a clipboard: I'd thought I'd finally get something dry to put on while I waited for Pedersen – who had gone with my keys and my instructions and my blessings to get me some other clothes – a hot cup of tea at least, but the clipboard was for me to fill out a form with all the requisite information for Joey. I dragged a sodden wallet out of my back pocket and fumbled through it for my Blue Cross card.

They left me the blanket, anyway, and found me a place to wait. The nylon lining of my jacket got colder and colder, but I didn't want to keep my overcoat on; it was already wet through where I'd sat on it. So I huddled on the edge of a gurney that might be taken away from me anytime, waiting to hear about Joey, waiting to warm up, waiting for Pedersen to show up with my clothes.

A siren ground to a stop outside and an instant frenzy at the doors caught my attention: none of it anything I understood, only that someone must be badly hurt. A gurney raced past with three people in attendance, trading terse medical comments. The injured man was no one I knew; he just added a new worry over Pedersen's safety to my circling thoughts. He wouldn't have taken the highway, would he?

Nearly an hour went by before a harried-looking resident materialized at my side. "OK, what did you give the kid?" he demanded. Not, are you Jamison, not even hello, just, what did you give the kid?

"Nothing."

"Jamison, right?" When I nodded, he snapped, "Won't wash. We know the boy was doped. What was it?"

My heart started racing. "But I didn't –"

"Can it, Jamison. Don't you know what happens when you sedate a child and leave him in the back seat of a car with no heater on?"

"It wasn't –"

"Second kid this week I've had with hypothermia because some jerkoff had to go have his fun and leave the kid in the car. The first one, sweet little girl just two years old, she died. *Died,* you hear me?"

"I hear you," I whispered. The chills came back.

"So now, what did you give him?"

"I don't know."

"Something you found on the street, hey? What color –"

"I mean, it wasn't me. Sergeant Hawley –"

"Lay off, doc," said a familiar voice. "He doesn't know anything about it, and the guy who does is out cold, maybe for good."

"Hi, Mack," I said weakly. I was glad he was in uniform, though he's big enough to back up anything he says, uniform or no uniform.

"Is the kid really in that much danger?" Mack asked, his hands coming easily up to rest on his hips.

The doctor looked a little confused. "This could be construed as child abuse, officer, I think I have to report –"

"I asked you, is the kid in that much danger?"

"Er – no, we expect full recovery, but –"

"Then bug off." Mack stared the doctor down. "It's this guy's son, all right, but he never, ever, did one thing to put him in here, check?"

"Er, no."

"Now, buzz off. I've got to ask him a few questions."

"Medical –"

"He can't give you any answers, so take your questions someplace else," Mack suggested. "And if you can't think of anyplace else, I'll name you a couple." He leaned one hand on the gurney I was sitting on and watched as the resident retreated in confusion. "Smart ass," he commented. "He knows damn well you had nothing to do with it. Likes to get his knife in and twist."

"He could just have been mistaken," I mumbled.

"Hell he was. I've gone around with him before." Mack looked me over carefully, from balding scalp to blue toes. "Well, you satisfied? I told you to stay the hell out."

"Yeah, and you said you'd keep me posted," I retorted. "What about that money Hawley had duplicated? I had to find out about that from your wife."

"What did it tell you?"

"Not much," I admitted.

"The last thing I learned was where these guys were getting together to pool their cash for their bonfire," Mack said., "Excuse me, I mean the holy fire of purification. That wasn't until damn near five o'clock. I had a lot of arranging to do, and then when I called you, you weren't home. So I left a message on the machine and went over there."

"That was you in the car parked up the street?"

"You bet." He eyed me up and down.

"Then, what do I find when I start tailing this crew but the same dark green Volvo wagon at the end of the line that I *know* was parked across the street from the house when I got there, and I *know* nobody came out of that house and got into it. Who's Lars Pedersen?"

"Guy I work with."

"Seen too much television," Mack complained. "He damn near ran me off the road with that trick at the Crosstown."

"You were following them, too?"

Mack blew an exasperated sigh into his mustache. "What do you think I do for a living, damn it, grow roses?"

"Well, hotshot, where were you when Pedersen and I got to the park? We followed the caravan in and nobody showed up for a good ten minutes, and then it was the guys from Bloomington. You lose him or what?"

"Guess."

I stared at him.

Mack raised his eyes to examine the cream-colored tile on the wall behind my head. "We're even for that little thing on Highway 12, that time back in high school."

I stared at him.,

"Washington's Birthday?"

I stared at him.

"Damn it, J.J., what do you need, words of one letter? You saw me take that skid."

"That was you?" Then I remembered: I'd taken one like that, on old Highway 12, the winter of our senior year. I'd laughed the whole thing off, driven straight on to the pizza place we'd been heading for, played the macho man. I was just lucky I hadn't shattered my kneecaps as they hit the pavement when I stepped out of the car. And I never did get up the guts to drive back home. "You got a lot of mileage out of that one." I almost laughed. "We're even?"

"Not quite. I drove over here." Mack grinned. "But when I got out to check your friend Pedersen's car – didn't you two jokers see me up the road when you turned around? No! Jeez, I'm glad you're not cops. When I got out of the car, it was a couple of minutes before I could get up the hill. And then all the fun was almost over."

Holy buckets, as Ferraro would say. I could sure be stupid when I wanted. "What do we do now?"

Mack sighed. "First, tell me how you got onto that meeting."

"Same way you did. Asked around."

Mack gave me a pitying look. "You expect me to believe that? I've heard how popular you are with that bunch."

"They're not the intellectual light of the universe, no," I said, answering his tone more than his words. "But I've got friends in between."

Mack nodded slightly, looking at the tiles again. "You got any other places to ask? There's Karen."

"Not your job, like you told me."

"Hell, it's not my job," Mack snapped. "Well, maybe I'll have to fight a little, but you think I'm going to let go of it?" He pursed his mouth, doing strange things to that mustache, and stared at the terrazzo floor for a moment. "Only trouble is, the only thing I can think of to do is work through you, and you've got problems galore, you might say."

"Like what?"

"You don't know yet, you'll soon find out," Mack said. "Can we put together what we do know?"

"You've got everything I had, considering tonight," I said.

"You want to know what they found in that car, besides Joey?"

"The money, I guess."

"The money. A cool half million."

I whistled, trying to imagine what it must have looked like tumbling out of a grocery bag.

"In used hundreds," Mack added. "Worth doping a kid for, or snatching his mother." He cocked his head at me. "There were a couple of telephones, too."

"Telephones?"

"One wall-mount, the kind that clips over a plug on a wall plate, and one with a jack. White trimlines, if it matters. And both of them with that gray gunk you get when you don't wipe 'em off very often."

"Telephones?" I repeated. I couldn't see what he was getting at.

"Think it over." Mack looked at me expectantly.

"Oh." What do you do to keep a mother chained to a house she might not want to stay in? Take away her kid whenever you go out. Take away the telephones so she can't call anybody. If the place is isolated enough, if all she can see is snow . . . if you take away her coat . . . "Clothes?" I asked.

"Coat, boots."

"What address did he give when he rented the car?"

"Good thinking, J.J. Eleven-eleven Nicolet, is what he said."

"Well, can't you go there and . . ." Mack started shaking his head. "Oh, it's downtown, isn't it? You'd have to get the Minneapolis . . ." Mack was still shaking his head.

"I guess it's a pretty big apartment building? Or a hotel? Is that the Leamington?"

"Nope. It's Orchestra Hall." Mack folded his arms and leaned against the gurney, which swayed against the wall with a muffled clank. "He had a driver's license with an address in Vermillion, South Dakota. We're checking that out now, but I didn't hang around to see what happened with it. I don't think he took Karen to South Dakota."

"Too far," I agreed.

"And across the state line. That'd bring in the FBI." He drew a deep breath. "They could have been called in, even so, with Joey involved." He spoke stiffly: not his case, and even the implied criticism was more than he liked to make. "The guy was doing his best with Joey, you can see that."

"Can I?" I asked, thinking of the resident.

"Sure. Had him wrapped up nice and warm. Didn't plan to be gone from the car for long, you know, and the night isn't that cold... he probably thought he'd be all right. It's the dope that cooled him down, kept him from moving around or waking up, the heater doesn't get into the back seat that well...."

I thought of what that might mean for Karen. Was she doped somewhere, cooling down? No, the telephones. She'd be in a house, at least, but if the heat had been turned off. . . .

"Here comes your pal."

Pedersen had appeared in the hallway, bearing a bundle of clothing under one arm.

"What kept you so long?" Mack asked.

Pedersen flicked a nervous glance at him. "I took the liberty of calling my wife from your house, Jamison, and little Gjerta wanted a story read, so I took a little time finding a book . . . *Peter Rabbit,* I hope you don't mind. I had to translate as I went along. What's chamomile tea?"

"Some kind of medicine."

"Oh, *camomile!* Yes, of course, the same word as at home. I told her castor oil, I hope that will do." He was setting out the clothes as he spoke; typically efficient (when he bothered to think about it), he'd brought my thickest sweater, wool socks, underwear and heavy trousers, my ski jacket and even a handkerchief. "I hope you don't mind the shoes," he said. "They looked the best choice." My joggers. Just that evening I'd been thinking that I should have dusted the rebounder to keep Karen happy. My eyelids clenched.

"Now all you need is a place to change. Jamison? Is something wrong?"

"No. Everything's fine. Thanks a lot, Lars. I really appreciate this."

Mack, going back on duty, as he phrased it, left with Pedersen. I found a men's room and stripped off my wet stuff and climbed into the dry things Pedersen had brought. My feet still felt like blocks of ice, but at least my legs were dry. I hit the hand dryer a few times and stood in its hot draft, warming up, closed my cold little fist around the coins I'd had in my pocket and went in search of a coffee machine.

A nurse in starched white pants and tunic found me sipping at a cup of lukewarm liquid and told me I could go see my son.

He was relaxed in a white crib, looking a little rosier than he had in the back seat of Hawley's car. They'd taken away his blue sleepers and dressed him in a tiny hospital gown from which his chubby arms stuck out straight to the sides. His mouth made a little sucking motion as I came up to the side of the crib. "He looks just like usual," I said.

"He should be fine," the nurse assured me. "The doctor's just letting him sleep it off, and then he'll probably want to keep him a little longer to make sure he's OK. He should be free to talk to you soon, I imagine." She found me a plastic bag to put my wet clothes in. "You could go home, I think," she said. "We'd call you when he wakes up."

I looked down the corridor. The lights had been lowered for night, and the walls were pale green, giving the hall an undersea look. My house would be empty, except for me, and my worries were splitting up and multiplying as it was. I didn't want to watch Charlie Chan catch crooks, or bits and pieces of old Johnny Carson shows, or anything else my television could provide, and my mind was rocketing around like the display on a video game, too unsettled for a book. "I'll wait downstairs," I said.

The nurse smiled and I lugged myself down the hall to the elevator that would take me to the first-floor waiting room.

I'd been dozing awhile when someone shook me awake.

"Oh, it's you," I said graciously.

The hairy detective plopped himself down in the chair next to me. "Glad to hear you got your son back, Mr. Jamison," he said. "Though the circumstances are a little confusing."

"Not really."

"Got it all sorted out in your mind?"

"Not much to sort."

"Then how about letting me in on it?"

I gave him a brief synopsis of Hawley's activities for the evening, and the idea I'd had from Mack's evidence – that Karen must be in some isolated house in the country.

"So now, all we have to do is find her," he said.

"Elementary, my dear Watson."

"Come on, Jamison, I'm doing my best for you. You don't have to get snotty." The detective produced the familiar notebook. It was labeled for use by reporters, I noticed, startled, just like the one Karen used to make notes for stories was labeled for use by stenographers. He flipped some pages and took a pencil out of a plastic pouch in his shirt pocket, just like the ones engineers use. *Now, there is a guy with an identity crisis,* I thought, but he seemed unaware of his plight, raising his big, Brezhnev-style eyebrows at his notes. "It might have helped if you'd told me about this meeting you attended tonight," he commented. "I don't mind meetings, I go to lots of them." He waited. I didn't say anything. "Tell me about it now."

"I just did."

"Not that. How you got onto it."

I sighed and explained about Ferraro. He nodded from time to time, but didn't write anything down, just made little checkmarks in his notebook. I got the idea it was an old story by now.

"You talked to your friend Forrester yet?"

"Yeah."

"He tell you about the South Dakota driver's license?"

"Just that Hawley had one in Vermillion," I said. "That fits with what I know – the first time I ever saw him was near Yankton, which is what? Forty miles away?"

"How long ago was that?"

"Four years, come April."

"That fits, too," the detective said. "They tore the building down three years ago, where this Hawley was supposed to live."

"You mean the license is false?"

"Just a little out of date. We've got the same problem right here in Minnesota," he added generously. He hadn't made any notes yet.

"What leads do you have to my wife, then?"

He looked past me at the sophisticated graphics somebody had caused to be painted on the wall of the lounge. "Not a damn one," he sighed. "Not one."

"The telephones?"

"Didn't have any numbers on them."

"The car?"

"Was rented. False address."

"I know that. I mean mud on the tires, fibers, all those things you read about in the papers."

"This is winter, Jamison. The guy had the car for about six hours and probably never went off a paved surface. As for fibers, so what? We already know he was in the car. We know he had your kid in there. We can go over it, and it's impounded, so we will if we have to, but even if anything could come of a search like that, it'll be a miracle, and it'd take weeks, months, maybe."

I stared at the carpet, a cheery little squared-off design in assorted dirt-hiding colors. A couple of years ago, a guy had kidnapped a woman and her daughter and kept them in his basement for weeks. The neighbors never noticed. Karen could get pretty hungry; I hoped Hawley had been keeping her where he was living, and there was food in the place. Once he didn't come back, she'd try to get out, wouldn't she? Find a pair of his shoes, a coat...

"He's been pretty thorough, so far," the detective said, as if my thoughts had been flashed on my forehead like headlines running around the old *New York Times* building. He sighed heavily. "I've got more bad news for you, Mr. Jamison. Some of our people are getting a little interested in where you might have been, couple of days last week. Like Tuesday or Wednesday, when this Chapin was getting killed."

"For Christ's sake!" I exploded. "I've already been through that once. Wasn't that enough?"

"Then there's this Wilmot. By your own admission, you were with him until maybe half an hour before he died. Doesn't take much to hotwire a truck, drive it fifty yards, sit and wait."

All I could do was shake my head.

"Now me, I don't see any reason why you should have done anything like that, unless you're a betting man, Mr. Jamison?"

I shook my head.

"Wilmot had a lot of winnings on him. Backs underdogs, and this weekend it paid off. Somebody might have been in for more than he could afford, but not you, right?" I shook my head again. "So maybe it ties in with this other thing you told me about when your wife was first missing, this object that you lost from your company? Because it doesn't seem like Wilmot's got anything to do with your family, now, does it?"

I shook my head again. Four crimes, Pedersen had said. Four, counting with his clear blue eyes. I'd been thinking only of one, the important one to me, and that one was far from being solved, as far from being solved as any of the others.

Next thing, I guessed, headquarters would start asking questions about Aunt Yuk, just as Burns had already done. I startled myself by laughing.

"What's funny?"

"Nothing. It's been a bad week."

The detective leaned back in his chair and studied me, but I didn't say anything else. I was tired, so tired I couldn't imagine ever feeling rested, and with him sitting right there looking at me I dozed off again.

At two in the morning, just like old times, somebody came to wake me up and tell me Joey was awake and I could go see him for a minute or two.

Chapter Twelve

He was standing up in the crib, holding onto the side and jouncing up and down when I walked into the room. I got a big grin and a "*Hi!*" that lit up my heart. "Hi," I said back. He held up his arms to be picked up.

"Can I?" I asked the nurse.

"Sure."

I picked him up and gave him a hug, and he nestled down against my side. "Where Mommy?" he asked.

"I don't know, Joe-Joe."

"Where Mommy?"

This could go on all night, or until he got an answer he liked. I looked at the nurse for help. "He talks well for eighteen months," she said. "He must be a bright little boy."

I smiled half-heartedly. "Where Mommy?" Joey asked.

"That's the big question, Joey," I said. The nurse cocked her head at me, clearly thinking this was a peculiar situation she'd like to know a lot more about. "They've both been missing for a week," I said.

"Where Mommy?"

"I don't *know*, Joey."

Another little face was turned toward me now, a face about four years old, on the other side of the bars of a crib, with wide brown eyes and a pinched little mouth.

"Maybe I ought to leave," I said to the nurse. She nodded. "Joey, kiddo, I've got to go," I said to him. "I'll come back and see you tomorrow, promise."

"Where Mommy?"

"She's wherever she is," I said soothingly. I began to try to pry his arms off my neck. "You stay here and sleep a little longer, OK?"

"No."

"Mommy will come and see you soon," the nurse put in, dripping honey. "You go to sleep now, sweetie, and when you wake up..."

I could have punched her. I don't believe in lying to little kids, especially not just to settle them down. I started to ease Joey into the crib and got a whiff of the powdery scent of his disposable diapers. "I'll see you tomorrow," I repeated. "You sleep now, OK?"

"Where Mommy?"

"Mommy's OK," I said, my voice trembling a bit. "I think so, anyhow. You go to sleep and I'll come see you tomorrow."

Joey plunked down on his bottom in the crib and stared up at me.

"Where's my mother?" the kid in the next crib over asked plaintively. The nurse gave me a dirty look I didn't deserve – who invited me to come up here in the first place? – and hurried over to the other kid.

"Bye-bye," I said to Joey. "I'm going bye-bye. I'll see you tomorrow."

"Bye-bye," Joey said disconsolately. "Where Mommy?"

I smiled as best I could and hurried out of the room, feeling like ten thousand species of rat. "You'll see Mommy very, very soon," I heard the nurse croon.

A doctor was bending over some forms at the nurses' station, an island of light in the dim corridor. "Mr. Jamison?" he asked, as I walked past with my head down.

I owned up.

"I'd like to keep your son another twenty-four hours, just to make sure he doesn't have any side effects from whatever he was given. That okay with you?"

This was a different doctor from the one downstairs, and I was a little confused. Grinning, he stuck out his hand and introduced himself as a pediatric resident. I told him, although I thought I had written it on one of the forms, who Joey's usual doctor was. He made appreciative noises. We established that twenty-four hours didn't mean that I had to come pick him up in the middle of the night; morning would do, "as long as it's by eleven-thirty," the doctor said. "We're just like a motel here, only more expensive."

"Fine," I agreed, and got into the elevator to go call a cab to go home.

As I stood in the glassed-in vestibule waiting for the cab and thinking of Karen, it occurred to me that she wouldn't have left my jacket and overcoat crumpled in a plastic bag, and I pulled them out and shook them. The printout of Pedersen's nosing into everybody's retirement fund fell out of the overcoat pocket onto the floor. Leaving it in the hospital for anyone to read didn't seem like the greatest idea in the world, so I shoved it back into the pocket. The cab pulled up to the curb.

"Jamison?" the cabby confirmed as I reached for the back door handle.

He permitted me to enter his cab and zoomed out of the lot just in time to catch the light turning from amber to red, which didn't slow him noticeably. The fine snow had started falling again; maybe an inch had accumulated on the sides of the road, lit yellow by the sodium lamps. The cabby pointed it out with great glee and regaled me all the way home with bloody exaggerations of the accidents he'd seen since it started snowing that evening, all the while looking to participate in one himself.

No one obliged, thank Heaven, and as he pulled up in front of the house he asked me who I thought would win the Superbowl.

"Redskins," I said. "Easy."

I guess he didn't agree: I had to argue him out of a seven-dollar tip on a three-dollar ride. The Minne-apple gets more like the Big Apple every day.

I fell into bed certain I would not be able to sleep more than two consecutive seconds and was out cold before the sheets were warm.

The phone brought me out of it. I groped toward the ringing, not sure who or where I was, and only realized as I picked up the receiver that the unusual light in the room came from the sun.

"H'lo?"

"Oh, J.J. what are you doing home at this hour?" asked Mrs. Eskew. "Not that it isn't wonderful to talk to you, but I hope you aren't sick? May I speak to Karen?"

"She's not here, Mrs. Eskew," I mumbled.

"Oh, dear, and I promised I'd call and tell

her all about Hawaii the instant I got in, only your house was dark last night so of course I didn't call then. When do you expect her?"

"I don't know, Mrs. Eskew. Karen's been kidnapped."

"Kidnapped!" I could picture Mrs. Eskew, not nearly so frail as she looked, staring into the phone receiver with her chin pulled back in disbelief. "Oh, dear," she said.

"Both of them. Karen and Joey. Only last night I got Joey back, but not Karen."

"Joey without Karen?" She paused again. "That doesn't make much sense, if you'll forgive me, J.J. How long have they been gone?"

"Since Wednesday afternoon."

"Not so long, then," she said comfortably. "Wednesday was only yesterday, you know. Time does drag when you're worried. . . ."

"Not yesterday," I interrupted, to get in before she went off on some tangent I had no hope of following. "The Wednesday before, last week."

"Oh." Mrs. Eskew paused. "J.J., would you mind if I come over and talk to you about this? I suppose you haven't even been cooking for yourself? Men! I can just see the dust!"

"Sure, come on over." The nightstand beside me was glowing with a sunlit layer of dust. She'll probably want to cook breakfast, I thought, swinging my legs out of bed and hunting around for my slippers with my toes. Sardines and beans on cornbread, I thought, picturing her banging through the kitchen cabinets in search of provender. Canned pineapple with tomato sauce.

I did her an injustice: she arrived about twenty minutes later with a bagful of breakfast-type groceries and started frying sausage and bacon in one pan and eggs in another, chipper as a chickadee. Karen counted my cholesterol and hadn't bought sausage in about four years. I almost drowned in my own saliva while I waited for it to be done.

"Now, I wonder," Mrs. Eskew said, when I had been served with enough food to satisfy her. "Do you know exactly when Karen was kidnapped?"

"Midafternoon," I said, mouth full. "Candy LeFleur saw her get into a red car with some guy –"

"A red car!" Mrs. Eskew sat up straight on the edge of her chair and stared at me. "My goodness, why didn't you say so? I saw her getting into that car, too, but I never dreamed she was being kidnapped! Why, I'd have run out with my pistol and put a stop to that, I tell you!"

I closed my eyes and said a brief prayer of gratitude that Mrs. Eskew had not realized that Karen was being kidnapped.

"I suppose you already had the car traced and know all about it," Mrs. Eskew said wistfully.

"Only that it was a late-model two-door red sedan."

"A what?" Mrs. Eskew laughed. "Hmmp. That Candy LeFleur has the eyes of a bat. It was a 1973 Duster – ten years old, and if you call that late model! Well, I don't."

"A '73 Duster," I repeated. "What was the license number?" I asked, a flat attempt at a joke.

"Mmmm, let's see. It started with DQS, I know that, because I thought of *deliquesce* to fit it, you see, and I was quite proud of myself. I wrote it down in my little notebook, but only the letters, I'm afraid."

"Deliquesce?"

"*You* know," Mrs. Eskew said, bobbing forward in her chair. "The game where you have to fit a word to the letters of the license number, in order, and shortest word wins?"

I gaped at her. Karen and I played that game, one she'd made up. She must have mentioned it to Mrs. Eskew at one time or another.

"And the rest. Mmmm. I'm sure there

was a seven in the number, because that's my lucky number, you see, and I was about to take this very long trip and I found it rather comforting to think of such a lovely word and have a seven in the license number."

"Yes." I stared at her stupefied.

"But it wasn't the first number, I know that, so it must have been the second, because if it had been the last, I'd have been disappointed, don't you know."

"A red 1973 Plymouth Duster, license DQS-something-seven-something," I said.

"That's right." She bobbed her head happily at me. "J.J., do eat your breakfast before it gets cold, there's a dear."

"Just a minute, Mrs. Eskew," I said. "There's a phone call I want to make first."

I tried for the hairy detective, with no more success than usual, and when I couldn't get him, called Mack. "Mack, you remember my neighbor, Mrs. Eskew?" I asked, when Joy got him to the phone.

"The old lady with the Luger? Hell, yes."

"Mack, guess what she –"

"She shot anybody, J.J., that's a 911 and you can let me go back to sleep."

"Shut up and listen. She's got most of the license number of the car Karen and Joey were kidnapped in."

"Now, that's something," he said. "You called the guy in Minneapolis, check?"

"Yeah, but he's not there."

"Okay," he sighed. "Give me the number and I'll call in and see what they've got."

"A '73 Plymouth Duster, DQS-something-seven-something."

"No numbers around the seven?"

"Sorry, no."

"It can only be one of a hundred, then," he said.

"Ninety. She'd have noticed another seven."

"Eighty-one, then, mathematician. Stay cool."

Mack hung up and left me counting on my fingers. Right. Eighty-one.

"Have I helped?" Mrs. Eskew asked, her pale old face thrust forward eagerly.

"Oh, yes," I said, with fervor. "You sure have."

"Then you can finish your breakfast. The sausage fat is already starting to congeal, and it's awful when it's cold, don't you think so?"

Like a dummy, I'd told the guy who took messages for the hairy detective that I could be reached at home, so once Mrs. Eskew got bored with stuffing food into me and went away I was left looking around for something to do. The TV offered me a choice of an *I Love Lucy* rerun, some blonde bouncing around in an art nouveau leotard, and a few less interesting things. I glanced through the paper, but I was too uptight to settle down to anything, except that I dusted the rebounder for luck.

My eye fell on the printout Pedersen had made the day before, and I remembered that even if I found Karen my troubles were far from over. One set of cops wasn't satisfied with my whereabouts for half of last week, although why they should pick on me I didn't know; and another set thought it peculiar that I'd had a drink with Mike Wilmot just before he'd been run over. I don't suppose I would distinguish myself with that crew by looking green at the thought. What kind of person deliberately runs over a rabbit, let alone a man?

Maybe something was to be found from the printout, after all, I hoped. I checked through the figures again: nobody at all suspicious, unless it was Pedersen, whose dossier didn't appear. I tried grouping the names by telephone prefix: a few people lived in the same general area as one another, but it was also the general area of the plant, so I couldn't make much out of that.

A date appeared after each address, which

puzzled me. My own was my date of hire, a year after I'd moved into this house. But others didn't match that way: I knew for a fact that Burns, to take the first example, hadn't been hired only ten months before.

Dummy, I told myself. It's the date personnel got the address. So Burns had moved, probably right after or before his divorce. Who else?

Wilmot (speedy they might be, but Pedersen had beaten them to that one before they blocked the records off) had moved a couple of years earlier. Two other guys, I remembered them bragging about their brand-new split-levels - one of them put a pipe auger through his plastic drain when he'd been in the house less than a month - and Fred Erikson, I'd helped him move... yes, those dates all matched.

I got out my map of Minneapolis, pushed the worn folds back together on the kitchen table, and began plotting my coworkers on it, feeling a little foolish. Joyce Amluxen lived in Golden Valley. Quite a commute. And Burns...

I stared at the map. Burns lived in an apartment on Riverlook Road.

I couldn't believe it. Twice I checked the little red numbers on the map that showed the building numbering system. Burns lived on Riverlook Road – and one step closer to the Mississippi, in the same block, was Bluff Towers, Chapin's apartment house. The buildings must be back to back.

The phone rang while I was still sorting out the implications. It was the hairy detective. "Oh, it's you," I said graciously.

"Did my guy get it right? Red '73 Duster, license DQS-something-seven-something?"

"Right."

He sighed. "I told you this was a bad luck case, Mr. Jamison. I checked that out. The Duster belongs to a lady I never heard of, no record, nothing to do with the case, nothing. Couldn't get an answer on the telephone –"

Of course not, you dunce, the telephones are both in somebody's property room.

"– so I called some neighbors. The woman hasn't been around for about a month, gone somewhere on business. Her brother's been looking after the place."

"Hawley?"

"Her name is Michock, and she's single."

"Divorced, maybe?"

"Could be. More likely the registration's out of date. Happens so often it's not even funny. She could have sold the car back last fall and the title hasn't caught up with the new owner yet. Costs the city a mint in lost ticket fines, that kind of thing."

"Yeah, sure. Thanks."

"I'll keep on it, but nobody around there seems to think anything unusual is going on. The house is in St. Louis Park, so it's only courtesy to let them know we're interested. I'll talk to your buddy."

"St. Louis Park?" But the line was already buzzing. It's not much fun to listen to an empty line, like they say in the phone book under "harassing calls," so I pressed the disconnect button and dialed a number I was surprised to discover I had to think about. More surprise: it rang. St. Louis Park, I thought, the disappointment so strong it was a physical pain in my throat. Too built-up for what Hawley had needed.

"Two-oh-three-nine, Pedersen," said a disembodied-sounding voice.

"Lars, it's J.J. I just stumbled onto something weird. You know that printout you did of the personnel files?"

Pedersen was in his pedantic mood. "Selected portions, Jamison. They keep the confidential information on paper."

"Selected portions. Enough. You know that R. Quentin Burns lives next door to Bill Chapin?"

"Good heavens." Pedersen sounded faint. "What do you suppose that could mean?"

"I've got no idea. But Chapin lived in

Bluff Towers, and Burns lives in the same block, on Riverlook Road."

"Rive –!" Pedersen stopped. "Jamison, evidently you are not coming in to work after last night's adventure. Can you possibly meet me for lunch? I . . . I know of someone else with that address."

"I promised Joey I'd visit."

"Do that first, by all means. I am flexible. Could you decide to indulge my taste for oriental food again so soon? I am thinking of that Vietnamese restaurant we spoke of once before. At, say, one-thirty?"

"Will do." I hurried into some clothes, blessed Pedersen for having the foresight to encourage me to leave my car in my own driveway the night before, and backed the vehicle through the two inches of partly cloudy on the drive. Ten-thirty. I could spend at least two hours with Joey, if they'd let me, I thought happily. Then I remembered the question he was sure to ask, over and over and over and over. The one I couldn't answer. Not yet.

Soon, Karen, soon, I thought, heading south. We've got a new lead, and Mack's working on it now.

I arrived at the Vietnamese restaurant with an insistent "Where Mommy?" ringing in my ears. From inside the door I looked over the dining room for Pedersen, but didn't see him. I explained to the host who wanted to seat me that I was to meet a friend, and he said, "Oh, you are Jamison?" with a smile and a bow. I bowed back and was escorted to a table behind a screen toward the back of the restaurant, in the no-smoking section. Pedersen was already ensconced in a red corduroy chair with a platter of various appetizers in front of him, of which I recognized egg rolls.

"You have been subjected to questions," he said, with a sharp upward glance at my face.

"Where Mommy?" I sat down opposite him.

"Yes. Precisely the most difficult sort to bear. I took the liberty of ordering, Jamison; be careful with that innocent-looking sauce in the dish with the red border."

A waiter had appeared out of nowhere with a warm plate and had deftly moved several items to it from the platter, using the chopsticks that had rested on it, and now went up in a puff of smokeless smoke, or seemed to. I cut into the egg roll with the edge of a fork, to Pedersen's amused disdain, and found it full of bean threads and vegetables.

"I thought we should be well clear of the office before we talked," Pedersen explained. "Did you bring R. Quentin's address?"

I pulled the printout out of my jacket and laid it on the table. Pedersen snatched it up eagerly. "Just as I had thought. Not only does he live but a stone's throw from Chapin's former residence, but he lives in the same building and on the same floor as Leonard Fink."

"Who?"

"The baggage handler, Jamison, who so conveniently retired on the day after Aunt Yuk began her adventure. I can't think why I didn't notice this yesterday. Too fixed on the retirement fund, alas."

I blinked at him. I blinked because my eyes were watering. My eyes were watering because of the sauce in the red-rimmed dish. I wondered if the blue-rimmed dish held a cooler sauce, but it looked for all the world like mustard.

"And the apartment numbers are quite close, numerically speaking, so I think we can assume a geographic proximity as well." Pedersen stopped to eat something and grinned. "I begin to see a pattern, do you?"

"Does your friend the baggage handler have a private trust fund, or did R. Quentin's wife walk away with the whole family store?" I asked, intending sarcasm.

"Don't be ridiculous, Jamison. Baggage handlers make almost as much as you do, and even you could afford a two-room in that building." Pedersen pointed his chopsticks at me. "Further, I have thought of something else. This push to finish Aunt Yuk began just before Christmas, did it not?"

"Mmmm."

"Suppose R. Quentin and this Leonard Fink attended a holiday party to which the persons who lived on that floor of the building were invited? Suppose further that at that party Mr. Fink mentioned his coming retirement? And the occupation which he would leave behind?"

"Possible."

Pedersen stopped to plunk his chopsticks into his rice bowl and emerged with a succulent lump of chicken. "One might postulate the following scenario: a manager, passed over for promotion by the company he loves –"

"He's just not as bright as Kochel, Lars, he ought to know that."

"He'd be a rare man indeed, in that case! Passed over, in need of money to placate a divorced wife and perhaps to impress a possible replacement for that wife, knowing that a valuable piece of equipment is in preparation and sure it can be finished by the date in question, he arranges with the retiring baggage handler to send the object astray. This he insures by specifying that it travel on an airline that will not permit it to travel as a person, and by choosing as an escort Bill Chapin, who is certain to relax one rule to suit another, particularly if the one he relaxes is only a general policy and the other is a direct instruction: not to miss that flight." Pedersen examined a black piece of mushroom and ate it. "How do you like that, hmm?"

"It's possible, I guess."

"No, I mean that dish. Which is it? Ah." Pedersen put his list back in his pocket. "The objective of this exercise, of course, is to produce either a ransom – unlikely, because too risky – or a payoff."

"Lars. Do you realize you're talking about Bob Burns?"

"You think it unlikely?"

"He's so . . . he's so gung ho."

"Spurned by his wife," Pedersen said, jabbing the air with his chopsticks. "Spurned, then, by the company that had his unquestioned loyalty. Unquestioning? Unquestioning."

"Spurned?"

"It must have been like sand in a newlywed's bed when Kochel got the division manger's job, don't you think?"

Possible. "What happened on the other end?" I asked. "After Lenny Fink put the case on the wrong plane, or whatever? Somebody there had to be in on it."

"Arvel Ripov, if that is his name."

"The private detective?"

"Who better?"

"Any of several thousand engineers in Silicon Valley, probably. That's wholly unfounded, Lars."

"Unfounded. Hmm. I have already mixed my mortar. That is the right word? And I plan to, what is it, start laying blocks for my foundation this afternoon." Something was missing: the old ready-to-do-battle gleam in his eye. He gazed at the chopsticks he was toying with. "I know of people, honest people in what might be viewed as vulnerable positions, who might have been approached by this Arvel Ripov as I believe Burns was, on one or another trip to confer with the contractor out there. That is one of the blocks. I can only hope that Mr. Ripov is a private entrepreneur, and not a representative of, shall we say, a larger enterprise."

Spies come in all brands, I remembered.

"Meanwhile, you will go and talk to Mr. Fink, to whom I have already apologized for calling a wrong number, not five minutes before you got here. You see, I learn from others, even your Sergeant Hawley."

I grimaced. "He might not be there."

But he was.

I'd been rehearsing my lines all the way over in the car, a good way to blow them when you make your entrance. But Lenny Fink was one of those jolly men who doesn't notice when you've blown your lines, or even if you had lines to blow. He greeted me at the door with a can of Stroh's in one fist and invited me in without even asking who I was.

"I just wanted to ask you a couple of questions about something," I said, turning down the mute offer of a can of Stroh's for myself. "It's about a package one of your neighbors sent to California."

"Oh, that!" Fink grinned, blue eyes laughing. "Damn fool thing, if you ask me. Did it work?"

"Work?"

"Yeah. It was supposed to keep the thing away from some kind of spy – I didn't understand it, but he's a good guy, Bob Burns, not like some I could name don't like people with the wrong occupation in the same building with them, as if my money wasn't as good as theirs. So I said sure, I'd do it."

A picture of a plain, friendly looking woman in her fifties stood on top of the big color TV, next to some pictures of people my age and a little older, some of whom looked like her and some more like the man grinning at me from the big chair he'd placed so he could see the TV. Stuck around the picture frames were little snapshots of smiling kids from infancy to maybe twelve years old. I felt like the world's worst rat.

"I'm not sure what you did," I said, waving away the can that had reappeared in Mr. Fink's friendly left hand.

"You're not one of those, what did he call them, industrial spies, now, are you? You're too late, the damn thing's been in California, let's see, two weeks."

I showed him my badge, so he could see for himself that I worked for the same company R. Quentin Burns did. "I just wanted to know exactly what you did for him, that's all."

"It didn't get lost, did it?"

"Well, it was misplaced for a while, but we've got it back, now."

"I told him it was a half-assed thing to do. All it was, was, day before I retired I looked for a black, lumpy-looking case coming down for Budjetair 101. I'd know it because it had one of those funny green stickers on it, you know, the poison thing? Mr. Yuk. And all I had to do was send it on a little late. I put it on a flight going out a few hours later, just the same as I do for Budjetair anyway when they've got an overflow. That way, anyone watching the guy who was supposed to be with it, see, would see him get off the plane in L.A. without it, and he could come back later and pick it up when they thought he hadn't brought it."

"Pretty clever," I said, meaning it.

"He tried to pay me, Burns did, but I told him, I don't need that, not for a favor for a friend."

"That was nice of you."

"I got enough money. I'm union. I went to visit my daughter in Florida last week, flew down and back, it's something, sitting there knowing just what's happening to the bags when the lady in the next seat is having little fits thinking hers are gonna end up in Seattle!" His smile turned self-satisfied. "Right there in Miami, just like they were supposed to be. I've flew before, but that was something."

"Florida must be a nice change, this time of year," I said incautiously. That did it. It took me forty-five minutes and a cold Stroh's fire-brewed before I could escape. One week of real retirement, and Mr. Leonard Fink was already a lonely man. I knew just how he felt.

I waited until amost five to go back to the plant, as Pedersen had suggested. Meanwhile I tried several times to get hold of Mack. No luck. I tried, not very successfully, to put Karen out of my mind as I climbed the stairs to meet Pedersen.

He was sitting staring off into space when I walked into the cubicle. "Ah," he said, coming back. "How did it go?"

"You were right."

Pedersen didn't look particularly pleased. "I, too, have confirmed the suspicions I spoke of," he said unhappily. "And I have another question. In the past, when you were a lead programmer, and there were schedule changes, haven't you had a copy of the memo that came down to Burns asking for changes?"

"Sure."

"So have I. But, Jamison, this time I am also a lead programmer. Aunt Yuk was shipped early, and I had no such memo. Nor had the hardware people."

"Might not mean anything," I said.

"And there is Mr. Fink."

Not much to answer to that. "Still, maybe there was a memo, and Kochel just told Burns orally, or Lisa slipped up distributing it, or Burns just forgot. . . ."

Pedersen smiled sadly. "Always the devil's advocate, Jamison. You have too little evil in your heart."

I let that pass. "What do you want to do now?"

"Look at Kochel's files."

"He's not due back from vacation until Monday, is he?"

"I propose only to wait until the unit is empty for the night. Let's go down to the cafeteria and have a quick supper while we wait."

"I'm still a little full from this noon," I said.

"Keep me company, then." Lars stood up and stretched. We went down the stairs just behind Burns, which gave me a peculiar feeling I couldn't identify. He didn't turn, and I didn't call out. Pedersen paused at the cafeteria door and watched Burns go on toward the guard desk. "That simplifies matters," he said, and pushed through the doors.

The cafeteria was on an economy binge that night, and Pedersen helped himself to the rice and bean casserole while I got us both coffee. At a table, he methodically buttered a roll and ate it in pieces torn off a bite at a time, then ate three or four kidney beans and the rice that clung to them. He pushed the plate away, shaking his head. "I can't," he said. He sounded surprised. "I am too excited."

He didn't look excited. He looked depressed. I sipped at my coffee, but even that was too much for me. I shoved the roll I had taken into my pocket and stood up.

"We will return separately, yes?" Pedersen said. "More natural, I think, and certainly less noisy."

"Okay."

"Who first?"

"I don't care. I'll go." I went down the hall and mounted the stairs as quietly as I could and walked past the dark frosted glass door of Kochel's office, and then Burns's, with a feeling of unreality. Even my own desk seemed strange when I sat at it and turned on the desk light that made up for the ceiling lights that had been turned off.

Pedersen appeared a few minutes later and eased himself into his swivel chair without the usual muffled clunk. *The light,* he motioned, and I turned it off. Somewhere a printer chattered for five or six seconds.

Pedersen held up three fingers: three others still working.

We waited in silence, for silence.

Somebody called a good night. He went past the door of our cubicle without a glance, headed for the stairs. When we heard his heels hitting the gritty treads, Pedersen stood up. I pantomimed a question.

"They are at the other end," he whispered, meaning that whoever was working would not have to pass us, or the managers' offices, to get to the stairs. Pedersen leading the way, we cat-footed it toward the dark office doors. He unclipped his badge from his shirt pocket to slip the lock on Kochel's door, and shut the door behind us with a soft click.

A faint light shone in from the parking lot, between the slats of the venetian blinds on Kochel's window. Pedersen moved to the window and closed the blinds tight. The beam of his pocket flash appeared, stiletto-thin, and he panned a five-inch circle down the fronts of the filing cabinets. I didn't see how he could slip those locks with a credit card. But Pedersen had come prepared: he pulled two small keys on a ring with a paper tag out of his pocket and twisted one of them in the lock of the second cabinet. I heard the lock release. We waited: no reaction from outside the office. "Lisa's much too careless," Pedersen whispered. He made only two false starts before finding the folder with Aunt Yuk's schedule in it.

The beam of the flashlight was only an inch across at close range, but that was plenty: enough to cover the words, "ship 2/1/83."

"But that's next week!" I protested, in a whisper.

"Exactly."

"You mean we beat our deadline by three weeks?"

"All unwittingly, and no bonus in sight," Pedersen agreed. "Look at this." He ran the flashlight across another piece of paper, a report by Burns on Aunt Yuk's status. She was "on schedule, barely, if no further delays occur."

"Further delays?"

The flashlight's circle bobbled as Pedersen shrugged. "I don't know what to do next," he admitted, still whispering. "Since Chapin is dead and you were sent to find him, I suppose you're also to take the blame for losing Aunt Yuk, but I don't know what evidence he has manufactured to support such a claim."

What could he claim? Burns must be the one who had shot Chapin, and now I knew why I had been chosen to find him. He must have been getting nervous, waiting for someone to find the body, must have hoped I'd put fingerprints all over the apartment, or maybe that I had visited Bill and done that already. But I had insisted on taking someone along . . . that could cut both ways, though. I'd also insisted on having a witness when we opened the apartment door. I could just hear the prosecutor: Isn't it true, Mr. Jamison, that at the time you didn't mention any sort of odor in the hall . . . ?

Wilmot? Observation, patience. I had eyes, I had patience. I had gloves to wear while stealing a truck. Nobody at home to give me an alibi. But that was the same night someone had tried to get into Pedersen's file, so . . . so what? If he's taken a terminal home, if he owned one, he could have done that from his own phone. He'd had time.

"I wonder if Burns signed out a terminal the night Wilmot was killed?" I whispered.

"One question among many. I think we'd better find some more answers while the opportunity is here." Pedersen clicked off his light and opened Kochel's door a crack and peered through it. Then he opened it the rest of the way and sauntered out, me after him, and closed the door and tested it to be sure it had locked.

"There was only one set of filing cabinet

keys," he mused. "I wonder if they'll work on R. Quentin's cabinets, too?" He cocked his head a moment, listening. "Wait here. I want to check something. I'll be right back."

He hurried down the hall and down the stairs, while I jittered in the bright fluorescent light at the corner of the passage that surrounded the cubicles and wondered what to say to anyone who came along. Six o'clock. Not time yet for Security to begin its rounds, but the printer at the far end of the unit's maze of cubicles fired another burst. At least one person still here.

Pedersen came soundlessly up the stairs and toward me. "He must be gone," he said. "He went down the stairs just ahead of us with his coat on, and he hasn't signed back in."

I drew a deep breath for a sigh of relief. "Shall we go fishing?" I asked.

Pedersen unclipped his badge for a second time and applied it to Burns's door. As a lead programmer, he had a faintly plausible reason to be in his boss's office after hours, so instead of the sneaking we'd done next door, he just reached out and hit the light switch.

"Come in, gentlemen," Burns said. "I've been expecting you."

The snicker I started at the TV-movie line

died. I know zip about guns, but the caliber of this one would have accommodated a fair-sized orange. At least, that was how it looked. In any case, considering that it was pointed at my stomach, I stood very, very still.

Chapter Thirteen

Big as it had looked at first, the hole in the end of the gun barrel expanded to the size of a cannon in the few seconds of silence that followed.

I could hear heels clack on the stairs so few yards away: the last late worker going down. If I shouted, what? Maybe both of us dead, Burns running down the long, straight lower hall past the guard's desk, out the doors. Sure to be caught, but what would it matter? If I turned, fled, would Pedersen be shot? Or would Burns run after me, down those stairs, down that long hall, get me or the guard coming to see what was wrong?

The sound of steps vanished abruptly, cut off as whoever it was reached the lower hall. "You'll want your coats," Burns said quietly. "Shall we go get them?" Pedersen nodded and turned slowly. "I'll be right behind you," Burns said. "You understand."

Pedersen strolled past me and down the upper hall toward our cubicle. "Stay a few steps behind him, Jamison, and a little to the left. That's right," Burns approved. "I want a clear shot at both of you."

As I walked, I studied the hall for possibilities. To one side, a long expanse of painted cinderblock. No cover but the water fountain and the coffee machine. To the other, the cubicles: a dash into someone's office, over the wall and into another, lead a chase through the maze and away down the steps and along that long, long hall with its stripes of light . . . but I'd be exposed crossing every wall, and what would Pedersen do? No way we could time it together, and Burns would just pick off whoever was left. Better not chance it. Leave that stuff for the guys on TV. I licked the sweat off my upper lip and kept walking.

"Against the wall, J.J.," Burns said. I spread my hands wide and leaned on the wall next to our door while Pedersen was allowed to get his coat. His face was ashen, but his eyes had the look they get when he's thinking about how to break some new computer code. It calmed me, that look. Pedersen came out and took a position that mirrored mine on the other side of the door, and then it was my turn to put on my coat and my boots and try to think. Not a damn thing I could use as a weapon in that office, not against a gun. Not one. I looked longingly at the telephone:

right about now, if my plans had gone right, I'd have been calling Mack to see what he'd found out about the Michock woman. I went meekly into the hall.

"Lars will go first," Pedersen said. "Just walk out at a normal pace. Have your badge ready to flash at the guard. Nothing else. Put your other hand in your pocket. Remember, you will be reflected in the door and I'll be able to see anything you do."

Pedersen began walking toward the stairs.

"Okay, J.J. Just like before, a little to the side and a couple of steps back. Good."

"Won't the guard think it's kind of funny? You holding a gun on us?" I tried.

"The gun will be in my pocket, but don't think I'd hesitate to shoot through it. I'll have plenty of money for a new coat."

Pedersen and I walked down the center of the concrete staircase, his steps soft, and I jingling after him in my galoshes. Burns was fairly close behind me and far to the other side of the stairs, to cover us both as we made the turn on the landing. I tried to think of what time it must be, whether Security would be making its first rounds yet. Not a chance. Or was there? When we turned into the first-floor hall, I could see the clock over the exit at the far end of the hall. I squinted. Couldn't make it out.

Pedersen kept to the center of the hall, walking with a slightly stiff, even pace past the orange doors of the cafeteria. I watched the light fall on his honey-colored hair, fade, light up again. The reduced night lighting hid nothing. I kept two steps back and to the right. Burns seemed to be about two yards behind me.

I realized that Pedersen was slowly angling to the right, and that made me nervous. What if Burns got jumpy? And then I saw why: a mop cart and cleaning buckets stood in the center of the rubber mat that crossed the lobby to the exit, and Pedersen was going to pass to the right of them, on the side toward the guard desk. There would be a couple of seconds when he would be between me and the glass doors, and both of us in full view of the guard at the desk. He wanted me to signal. What signal?

Burns shifted slightly to the left. We must make an odd procession, I thought, three men with our fists in our pockets, not speaking.

The guard's name was in the duty slot on the front of the desk: Joseph Rasniewski. A Joe, like me. Good omen? I did the best I could: as Pedersen detoured around the mop cart I said loudly, "Good night, Joe," and extended my badge in my left hand for him to see, well down and toward the right, and made trigger-pulling motions with my forefinger. I couldn't see myself in the door, and I couldn't see Burns, either. I bit my lip and stuck my right index finger out straight, like a gun in my pocket.

"'Night, Mr. Pedersen," Joe said. "'Night, Mr. Jamison. 'Night, Mr. Burns."

Pedersen and Burns mumbled something. Both sounded strained, Pedersen in particular, and I hoped Joe Rasniewski heard it in their voices, too. When I got to the outer door, I glanced at the glass panel to my right and saw the guard reflected, with his magazine in front of his face again. Well, they were hired more for brawn than brains, I reminded myself. Tough luck.

"We'll take your car, J.J.," Burns said. "I don't think it handles as well as Lars's. Less temptation to do any tricks."

"I'll have to lead," I said.

"Of course. Why should I mind? I don't have to bother about the coat pocket now, do I?"

Pedersen and I revolved around each other while walking forward, like the two balls of a bolas. That made Burns the gaucho, I guessed, and almost laughed. Nerves.

The Fairmont sat on the other side of an expanse of snow-covered rectangles surrounded by warmer, wet pavement, two or three minutes' walk away. I wondered what I could do in that time, in this wide-open space. The lot was well-lit, to the comfort of female employees, and I'd heartily approved of the change when it was made. Just now I wished I worked for a less progressive company.

We got to the Fairmont without the creative engineer that worked for a progressive company having thought of any solution to his current problem. I unlocked the door.

"Bullets go through glass," Burns reminded me. "Get in and unlock the far door. I will go around with the gun very close to Lars. If you try any tricks, I will shoot him. Then I will shoot you."

That seemed clear enough.

I leaned across the seat and pulled up the locks on the two far doors and got myself upright behind the wheel. Lars got in. Burns got into the back seat, locked the door and slid across, and the gun cozied up to the back of my neck.

"Neither of you can afford to have J.J. die at the wheel," Burns said. "So I suggest no sudden moves. Please don't put your seat belts on." I heard the buckle of his seat belt click shut. Lars turned his head slightly: the buckles in his Volvo were a two-hand operation. Trust us Americans to have the edge when it comes to eliminating exercise.

The car complained loudly that I had started the engine without fastening my seat belt. After half a minute or so it gave up and shut up. I moved slowly out of the parking place.

The bright blue-white lights on the tall standards gleamed over the few cars left, shifting reflections as we moved forward. No engines coughing awake, no headlights coming on. Nothing. *Nichts. Nada.* It occurred to me that for four years I had been missing a marvelous opportunity to learn a Scandinavian language. Tomorrow, right after I got Joey settled, I'd –

Stop thinking about it. The headrest behind me slammed down against the seat, and I jumped. The gun pressed into the back of my neck, in the notch of my skull just where it joins my spine. Bad place for it, I thought, and licked my salty upper lip.

Stop thinking about it. The lot of the bar across the road was full, even on a Thursday night, and the car dealer had all his lights and balloons and automatic hoopla going, but no customers. We passed Arby's. Not my favorite restaurant of all time, but I'd miss it, I wanted lunch there tomorrow, after Mack and I –

Stop thinking about it. The gun was right where it had been since the beginning of time. "Where are we going?" I asked.

"Straight. Turn up your dash lights, I can't see how much gas you've got."

I reached slowly for the knob and turned it. Half a tank, R. Q. Plenty to take us to some dark spot in the semi-country where you can do us in. And what will you do about the car? The road ahead gleamed dark, and water rattled against the underbody of the Ford as I sliced through the puddle. The quiet afterward came as a shock. The car. Burns would drive my car, my five-year-old, visible car that I had driven so many times and Karen had driven so many times right back to the lot where I had parked it so many times, lock it up tight and drive home in his own. Keys down a sewer grating. Dust off the hands.

"What will you do after this?" Pedersen asked musingly.

"I've got my escape hatch," Burns said. "Sorry to disappoint you, but even I can think ahead. But actually, I plan to go on just as I have, in this job. Nobody will link me to any of this."

I made a superhuman effort and did not

mention Lenny Fink, who deserved better neighbors in his retirement years.

Pedersen shifted a little, slowly, and looked back at Burns. "What will Kochel think, when he discovers that you shipped so early?" I wondered if Pedersen could see that the gun was resting steadily on the headrest, jabbed into my neck.

"Not a damn thing," Burns laughed. "I arranged that long before he went on vacation – he thought it would make us look good, after that last little leak we had. I'll get a bonus, if anything. How can I help it if Chapin was careless?"

"That leak to the Japanese last summer was you, too," Pedersen said.

"Testing out Arvel," Burns affirmed.

"What will Kochel say about Aunt Yuk being cut?" Pedersen pursued.

"She wasn't. Arvel rewrapped a few wires, splattered a little solder around. Very neat. Hardware looked her over and decided nothing essential had been compromised, some amateur had had a look and couldn't have figured out what he saw."

"What was the object of that?" I asked, curious in spite of the pressure on my neck.

"When we get a buyer, and I turn the plans over to Arvel, Kochel will figure

Wilmot was wrong, somebody who knew what he was doing did get in."

So that was why Wilmot had to go. And the plans weren't sold, then. Could I believe that? Could I believe Burns hadn't found any spooks from the KGB with their greedy little hands out?

"For that matter, he may never find out anyone got the plans at all." Burns sounded gleeful, but I didn't like being told all this, didn't like the implication that my fate was sealed. I had other things to do; a kid waiting for me to take him home and a wife to find. I didn't need Burns and his fantasies.

"I see a little shopping center up ahead," Pedersen said. "Could we look for a pay telephone? I would like to bid farewell to my family."

"How stupid do you think I am?" Burns asked. The gun jumped against my neck as he laughed. "Even if I spoke Danish, I wouldn't let you do that." He kept laughing, short harsh bursts that made the back of my neck cringe. A pain started there, in the tense muscles, and spread rapidly over my head. "What about you, Jamison? You want to call your wife?" Burns asked, through his laughter.

I didn't answer. The chuckles stopped, after a while.

"I don't think you're stupid," Pedersen said into the silence. "But I do think you may have failed to consider every facet of your plan."

"What's that supposed to mean?"

"Think about it." Pedersen turned his face away, to look out the side window as the little shopping center slid away behind us and the dark pressed in. Burns said nothing. The nose of the gun pushed a little harder into the back of my neck. It was warm, now, already stealing the heat of my body. Ahead of us a light turned red.

"Stay in the right lane," Burns said, I slowed and let the car roll to a stop. As a car came up beside me, I turned my head automatically: the gun jabbed at my neck. I looked forward again.

"I still don't see," Burns muttered.

Didn't see that four bodies might get in the way of his keeping his job. Didn't see that he'd left a trail a mile wide for anyone who wanted to look, and that after this, a lot of people would be looking hard. Forgot that the three of us had left the plant together, for instance. That Lenny Fink knew what had happened to Aunt Yuk. That Chapin lived just around the corner, but he'd sent two men several miles to check on him. That he'd selected Budjetair.

"*I* never got any flack from the others," he said. "Small stuff but the same in principle."

Didn't see that he couldn't possibly keep his job and go on making money on the side, selling company secrets.

"Merrill," Pedersen said. The gun jerked.

Merrill had been fired four months before, for cause, the cause being that he had supposedly turned over some small secret procedure to a competitor.

Burns didn't reply. The cars ahead of me moved forward as the light finally changed, and I slowly followed them. Nobody had even thought of Burns in Merrill's case. There'd been a third small leak; Chapin had been suspected of that. I wondered if Burns had tried to set him up on this one, too, and failed. Maybe Chapin had figured it out. Maybe I was just Burns's fallback position.

"I never would have believed it of you, Bob," I said. "Of all the guys in the unit, you've always seemed to be the one with the most company loyalty."

"I was loyal to them," he snapped. "They weren't loyal to me. *My* marriage broke up over the hours I worked, and they cheated on my overtime. They promoted Kochel over my head, and left me at the same salary three years running when everyone else got raises – why shouldn't I make a little extra money, especially now that I have to pay half of my income to Angela?"

A proverb my father liked to quote flashed through my head: "He who once a good name gets, may piss in bed and say he sweats." No, nobody would have suspected Burns, if he had let well enough alone. But there was a good reason that he hadn't been promoted: Burns lacked the edge that Kochel had, the knack for seeing one step farther than anyone else, one step faster. That was why he was still where he was, a unit manager. If Kochel had taken it into his head to sell Aunt Yuk, nobody would ever have known she'd been compromised. I could see a couple of better ways to do it myself.

But Burns had tried to get fancy. Burns had thought of an elaborate scheme involving retiring baggage handlers, cheapo airlines, an impetuous employee . . . and now he had two murders behind him and a gun at the back of my neck, when all he'd have needed to do was borrow the key to the Xerox out of Lisa's desk, instead of hoking up this solid-shit kludge.

"I figure if I shoot Lars running," Burns said, "and you close up, it will look like you tried to cover yourself, and then out of remorse . . ." He stopped. Maybe he was seeing that it couldn't work. Maybe, maybe, he'd decide to just split, leave us alone and on foot while he dashed for his escape hatch... Pedersen moved slightly. He had just been given the chance to save himself. I glanced admiringly at his dark blue overcoat, and then I remembered the snow.

"Doesn't it bother you to have two murders on your conscience?" Pedersen asked, much as he might have asked, "Do you know you have a spot of spaghetti sauce on your tie?"

I could feel Burns shrug: the gun moved. "I don't mind," he said carelessly. "They weren't the first. I don't like bayonets, though, they're too messy."

If you can keep your panic down, your body functions automatically. My eyes had been following my ordinary driving routine: glance side to side of the road ahead every couple of seconds, check the mirror maybe every ten. Now the mirror showed a flashing red light.

"I have to pull over," I said. "There's a red light behind me."

"No, Keep going."

That was bad news; he wasn't thinking clearly, was beginning to panic himself. I felt the gun shift again as he turned in his seat to check behind us.

"It would be less conspicuous to pull over," Pedersen remarked. Ahead of us, a car headed for the shoulder. We passed it.

"He can get by in the passing lane," Burns said. "Just keep it nice and steady, hear?" The warm nose of the gun again pressed firmly into the notch at the bottom of my skull. The inside of the car pulsated with red light, the siren drowned out whatever Burns was saying; the cop – it was a cop – was sitting right on my tail.

"Why the hell doesn't he get by?" Burns shouted. "Just pretend you don't see him."

Sure. "He wants me to pull over."

I could feel the sweat rolling down my sides, clammy under my T-shirt. "I guess you'd better," Burns shouted. "Don't argue, just take the ticket. Say you didn't notice him."

I flicked my turn signal and got over onto the shoulder. The cop was right behind. He pulled up maybe a car length back with the front end of his car sticking out into the road. I glanced at the mirror, but he had aimed his spotlight right at it and the inside of the Ford was almost floodlit, the mirror blinding. I half-reached to flip it back, get that light out of my eyes.

"No," Pedersen said softly, into the silence after the siren died.

Right. Show him the gun Burns still had at my neck.

Nothing happened.

"Where the hell is he?" Burns asked, turning around. "What the hell's he doing? He doesn't want you, get going again, J.J."

With a quick, unformed prayer, I popped the clutch. The car lurched forward a couple of inches, and the steady ticking of the engine died in a rattle.

"Shit, can't you even drive?" Burns demanded. "Get the fucking thing moving."

I'd been pumping the gas pedal as hard as I could, and now I turned the key. The starter motor gargled. The aroma of gasoline filled the car. "You're making me too nervous," I said. "I've flooded it."

The gun left my neck, leaving behind a cool spot I automatically rubbed with one finger. Burns locked the doors. A second squad car pulled in ahead of us, this one angled over the shoulder in the opposite direction. The dome light glinted briefly as the cop got out. "Where is he?" Burns asked.

I felt more than saw Pedersen turning in the seat beside me. The cop in the front car had disappeared. Crouching behind his car. I began to slide down in the seat, a fraction of an inch at a time. Two shadows got out of the car behind us and moved forward slowly, one on each side.

Burns turned from side to side, trying to keep both men in view at once. "Goddamn it, J.J.," he said through his teeth. "You klutz! Act normal, hear? I don't want anything tipping them off. Nothing."

I wondered where the gun was.

The cop on my side came up to the window and tapped on it. I began to roll it down. In the light of his spotlight I could see sweat on his forehead and I thought, *He knows, he knows what's going on!* I glanced down at his right side and saw the gun loose in the holster, ready for action, his hand hovering over it.,

Burns moved.

At the same moment, Pedersen threw himself sideways across the car, through the space between the front seats. A small, terrified moan. The gun went off. My ears exploded with pain. I huddled down in the seat, feeling it jerk with the struggle I couldn't see or hear. Something brushed by my head and the struggle stopped.

"Drop the gun," I heard faintly through the ringing. "Come out slow." The bitter, burned taste in the air made me cough. My mind winged back twenty years, to sit on the sidewalk banging caps with a stone, and forward again to Burns crawling out of the back seat, Pedersen pulling back to collapse into the front seat, my own sweat running into my eyebrows.

Burns was spread, spiderlike, against the side of the car, and as the ringing in my ears started to fade I heard the cop on the passenger side asking Pedersen, very politely, to please step out for a moment.

My turn next. I followed directions and made my shaky way to the squad car that had angled in front of mine. The smell of melting snow was almost unbearably sweet, after the hot, burnt stink of the car. The cop opened the passenger-side door for me and invited me to sit. I sat.

He got in on the other side and communicated with his radio. I'm alive, it occurred to me. I'm alive. Pedersen's alive. They've got Burns, and Pedersen and I are alive! I wiped my face on the scratchy sleeve of my overcoat. "How did you know?" I asked.

"We got a call."

Very informative.

They got three calls, I learned later. One from the security guard at the plant, a man not nearly so stupid as I'd feared. He'd thought it was strange for three men who worked together to walk out in a spaced-out line, instead of in a bunch. Then he saw my signal, saw the blockier shape of Burns's pocket, looked up the makes and license number of our cars and called the police to say what he thought was happening. He thought Burns was taking his own revenge on us for selling the pattern discriminator, but that was close enough that somebody had come to check the lot and found two of the cars still there.

A woman who wouldn't give her name had dialed 911 from a pay phone to say that she'd seen a light blue Ford headed north with three men in it, and the man in the back seat had seemed to be holding a gun to the driver's head. How had she seen all this? the dispatcher had wanted to know. She'd had plenty of time to look while they stopped beside her at a traffic light. The man with the gun hadn't bothered to conceal it. Pretty exciting, huh? She hoped they got there in time.

Thank you, lady, wherever you are.

The third came from a concerned citizen who traveled with a radio to which he listened for police calls, his normal purpose for doing so unspecified and his name likewise in oblivion, who had seen the car answering the description he'd heard and was happy to let the police know just where it was and in what direction it was going.

Concerned citizen, may you never be cited for speeding.

I got home very late, with no car. The hole in the roof was evidence, and naturally enough the hole was no hole without the car around it, so . . . they'd let me know when I could have it back.

The telephone answering machine contained just one message, from a male who didn't identify himself: "Jeez, J.J., now what did you get yourself into?"

Mack, of course. He sounded even more pained than usual.

Chapter Fourteen

Mack waited about four hours to attack the telephone lines again, and woke me out of a stunned sleep. I wasn't in bed; I'd sat down on the couch to try to figure out what to do with Joey once I got him from the hospital and to worry about how to find Karen, and I'd dropped off.

"OK, sport," he said. "I'm off duty. Want to go have a look at that house?"

I rubbed my eyes against the inside of one bent arm and yawned. "House?"

"The one where the red car was registered." Mack sounded disgusted. "The lady's driver's license lists her there, too. If she's gone, maybe one of the neighbors can tell us where she went."

"Sure." I leaned my swimming head against the side of a cabinet. "Just let me brush the fur out of my mouth, huh? I fell asleep on the couch last night."

"See you in ten minutes."

The kitchen clock said just before seven. The sky outside the back window was just turning the bruised pink that comes before dawn on a clear day. I let the water run until it was hot and put some on to boil for a quick cup of coffee, wiped off my sticky feeling face with a damp paper towel, and prospected for dry cereal in the cupboard, only to find I'd eaten the last of it.

For luck, I shaved and took out the garbage that had accumulated over the past few days, and when Mack arrived on the dot of 7:07 I was just walking out to the curb eating chunks of pineapple out of the can.

"Look at you," he said. "Now we know who's civilized in your house. Get rid of the can, will you? I don't need it in my car." He was still in uniform; he must have come straight from the station, I figured.

I ditched the can in the trash and tucked the spoon into my jacket pocket. I should have called Lisa and told her I won't be in, I thought, and then remembered that Lisa didn't get to work until eight. Well, who would care? My boss sure wouldn't.

"You got yourself in the paper, you know that?" Mack said. "Name, address, everything, even the hole in the roof of your car. I don't know why your phone hasn't been ringing off the hook."

"Nobody up yet, I guess." My stomach rumbled against the very idea of black coffee and canned pineapple for breakfast. My hands were icy again, as they'd been so often this mild-weathered week.

"Nine days. She'll be hopping, I'll tell you, J.J."

"I hope so."

Mack's little blue Honda splashed down the hill and made the turn onto Xerxes. We followed a school bus that made a left onto 42nd Street, stopping every time the red lights went on and the stop sign swung out to the side, which happened every other block. I'd see the kids lined up at the curb, and then Mack would pull up close enough to the bus to get us asphyxiated, and the bus would move away, leaving the corner looking as if a giant vacuum cleaner had come along and sucked up the kids. I pushed my fists together in my lap. Someday Joey would be getting into one of those yellow buses. Would Karen be there to wave good-bye, like the woman in the rust-colored bathrobe standing in the window of a corner house, fourth time we stopped?

Mack glanced at me. "Stay cool," he said.

He didn't like this. He didn't like going it on his own. Or maybe he did: I'd seen him do things before that didn't quite fit with the image of the by-the-book cop. But he didn't like going it with me: I was untrained, unprofessional, involved, therefore unreliable.

His ambivalence was like an odor in the car.
"I'm cool," I croaked. I was. I was freezing and sweating at the same time. "You haven't heard anything about Hawley, I guess?"

"Sure I did. Think I like wild-goose chases? I called the hospital before I called you. He's still out, and nobody's guaranteeing that he'll wake up." Mack gave the school bus the finger as it turned off our route.

"Those people get their money back?"

"Sort of. They've got receipts."

I tried to imagine owning nothing but a few clothes and a receipt. People living under bridges, and there were plenty of them, at least had an old mattress, a pot to cook in, maybe a book or some magazines.

We crossed France Avenue into St. Louis Park, and Mack brightened up. He was on his own turf, now. "The Minneapolis guy said licenses and registrations are out of date sometimes," I said.

"Well, we just hope."

We hit Excelsior Boulevard and waited for a light. Mack turned left, past the Miracle Mile, and swung onto the ramp for Highway 100 north.

"How far is it?"

"How far can it be? This isn't Alaska, even when it feels like it." Mack kept to the right, stopped for the light at 36th Street, where a crumpled guard rail gave vivid evidence of another accident, braked in a flurry of pushes as someone pulled in ahead of him on the other side of the intersection, pulled over into the exit for Highway 7.

"You going to stop at the office?"

Mack shook his head. "I got everything arranged with them. This is just the way we go."

"What does the Minneapolis guy think?"

"He'll be glad to cross you off his list, believe it."

We headed west on Highway 7, and Mack soon turned off into a residential area. I was surprised: somehow I had pictured Karen being held out in the middle of nowhere, with no one likely to see her if she went for help, no neighbors to come to a door she pounded on, nothing but snow . . . this was just a residential street, ordinary houses, not in each other's laps but close enough for a shout, a wave. "It doesn't look too hopeful, does it?" I asked.

"Don't give up before you begin." Mack slowed the car to a crawl, checking house numbers. "There we go," he said, and pulled over.

I wanted to rub my eyes. The house was in the middle of the block, and sat squarely in the middle of its lot, giving it about thirty feet on either side between it and its neighbors. It couldn't have been more everyday: the kind the real estate people call a Cape Cod conversion, painted a sedate gray with white trim and maroon storm sash and a maroon front door on which a white-frosted wreath of pinecones hung. The only odd thing about it was the chainlink fence, maybe four feet high, that surrounded it well inside the lot line, and the sign on the gate, BEWARE OF DOG. Somebody meant it, too; they'd taken a snowblower to the four or five feet inside the fence and dug it out just about down to the grass. "Mack, this can't be it," I said. "Are you sure?"

His eyes roved over the house, marking whatever professional points there were to be marked. "It's the right address," he said.

Next to the house, but outside the fence, was a detached garage painted a matching gray. The driveway hadn't been cleared since the last snow, two nights before, and the surface of the snow had turned lumpy with melting. A second gate, with a padlocked chain holding it shut, completed the fence next to the garage. I looked at the windows. Someone had left the drapes closed; they hung in straight folds over the glass from top to bottom and side to side, giving the house a blinded, introspective air. All the drapes matched, so I guessed they were lined. That would account for the opaque look.

"Well, let's see what we can get." Mack sounded disappointed. He got out of the car, and I reluctantly released my seat belt and got out after him. He stood on the sloppy sidewalk another few seconds, looking at the house, before he moved to the front gate. "Must be some dog," he said, pointing down. The gate had a heavy-duty latch operated by foot pressure from the inside. Mack reached over and tugged at it, but the angle was all wrong for the leverage and he gave up.

I followed as he walked around the corner of the fence to the garage, leaving ragged-edged footprints in the slush on the driveway, and put up his hands to look through the glass of the garage door. "We got something," he said. I looked into the garage myself. There was the red Duster with the *deliquesce* license plate.

I heard a low growl to my left.

A thin-looking Doberman stood stiff-legged inside the back gate. It sure looked like a dog to beware of, and I took an involuntary step back.

"Not barking," Mack said. "Probably serious." He looked past the dog at the house, maybe ten feet away. "Tear the ass off you before you got to knock on the door. Friendly folks."

A door opened on the other side of the driveway, and a woman called out, "Don't mess with that dog, mister, it's trained to attack."

Mack turned toward the woman. She was fifty or so, a little on the stocky side, wrapped in a flowered housecoat. "Thanks," he said. He gestured at his uniform. "Can you tell me anything about the people who live here?"

"I don't know," she said, half to herself. "You a real cop? You got some kind of ID?" She shut the storm door and the latch clicked. Taking no chances.

Mack produced a card with his picture on it, climbed the concrete steps and held the card and his badge up to the spot she rubbed clear in the condensation on the glass.

"Just a second," she said. The inside door shut.

"What's she doing?"

"Calling the cops." Mack rocked on his heels, looked at the garage, at the gray house, at the dog still standing with ears pricked inside the fence. It danced a little under his glance and growled again. I looked at the windows, curtained in a kitcheny-looking fabric, but just as opaque as the ones in front.

A trick of the light, I figured. The sun was barely up.

The door of the house next door opened. "Come on in," the woman said, holding the storm door ajar. I crossed the sloppy driveway and the shoveled one that belonged to the other house and climbed the concrete back steps. Mack had been careful to wipe his feet, so I did, too. "That's Emily Michock's house," the woman said. "She's been away for a long while, though."

"How long?"

"Oh, since just before New Year's. She's on assignment for something, in Africa, of all places, and she won't be back until the end of the month." The woman looked worried. I could see that she didn't like something about that house next door, just the way she kept glancing out of the window at it, and I began to have a little hope.

"Who shovels her snow, feeds that dog?" Mack asked.

"Oh, she's got this guy staying there to look after the house, and he's doing some remodeling for her while she's gone. He does the shoveling – snow-blowing, really."

"What does he look like?" I asked.

"Tall and thin. And funny eyes. I don't know how Emily could trust anybody with eyes like that."

I wanted to run across the two driveways and throw myself through one of those dark kitchen windows before the dog knew what was happening, but instead I stood still. Mack glanced at me.

"What kind of remodeling is he doing?" he asked.

"*I* don't know. But I can tell you, Emily won't be pleased. He's been bringing in sheets and sheets of plywood, this awful splintery-looking stuff, and old two-by-fours and it looks cruddy, I'll tell you, and Emily's a pretty particular woman about things like houses, even if she does have some peculiar ideas about other things."

What ideas, I wanted to ask, but Mack was going in a different direction. "Is the dog hers?"

"That dog? No! The fence is hers – the neighbor kids were always letting Mitzie out of the old one and she'd run all over and come back filthy, you know how dogs are, but Mitzie's just the *nicest* little poodle! And that's another thing, I don't know what that man can have done with her, oh, I'll tell you, if I knew how to reach Emily I'd call her up in a minute, even if it is all the way to Africa and costs practically three dollars a minute, and that dog is a *menance,* why, I'm almost afraid to take out my garbage for fear it will get loose, and if I only knew how to get hold of Emily, well – I'd call her right up, that's what I'd do."

"Is there just the man living there?" Mack asked. I braced myself for another flood.

"Well, I don't know if even he's there, still. I haven't seen him the last day or so. And I don't know. Sometimes he has a little boy with him, I guess it could be his son or something, only I never saw the little boy until maybe a week ago or so, and the dog doesn't know the boy, I'll tell you that, because this man comes out of the house and chains the dog to the fence, you can see where he has a chain on the fence, and then he carries the little boy out to the car and then he goes back and lets the dog loose in the yard, I think it's criminal, I really do, but with all the divorce these days it could be just his son visiting, I guess – but he carries the boy out to the car and then he *lets that dog loose,* and I will tell you that dog is a real menance, I always check to be sure both gates are shut before I even open my front door to get my newspaper. If I just knew how to get hold of Emily! I'm so glad somebody is finally paying attention."

"Have you called the police?" Mack asked, surprised.

"No, but I did call my councilman and he

said he couldn't do anything if the dog was fenced in and hadn't attacked anybody and I think it's a *shame* everything has to wait until somebody gets hurt, I really do, it could be a *child*, and I called Animal Control and they wouldn't do anything either. How do you like that?"

I stepped over to the window and pulled the cheery red-plaid curtain aside. Halfway down the drive, there was a short length of chain attached to the fence. The dog, still bristling on the back walk, was wearing a choke chain.

"I wish I knew what happened to Emily's nice little poodle," the woman said disconsolately.

"Probably this guy felt like he needed a watchdog and put the poodle in a kennel," Mack suggested.

"A kennel! Oh, poor Mitzie! She's a people dog, officer, she wouldn't be happy *at all* shut up in a kennel! If I only knew *where* in Africa Emily is, I'd call her up in a minute. But Africa's bigger than you might think."

I had a horrible feeling Mack was about to pursue this bit of geographical information. "What's she doing there?" I butted in.

"Why, Emily's an investigative reporter. She's on assignment."

"What does she investigate?" I asked, before Mack could get his foot in.

"Flying saucers." An infinitesimal pause followed. But she was instantly in full spate again: "She's not exactly a kook, Emily isn't, but she does have this interest, and she goes all over where there might be flying saucers and she writes them up, only not under her *own* name, you know, there's a lot of danger in that, she says, she uses her grandmother's maiden name so nobody will know who she really is –"

"What name is that?" I interrupted.

"Well, I'm not sure I should tell you." I pulled out my wallet and found one of my CATCH business cards and handed it to her. "Oh, I guess that's different. She's Astrid Astridsdatter."

I nodded. Emily was a kook.

"Can I use your telephone?" Mack asked.

"Well, but Emily –"

"I just want to call the station," he said, "to get a dog handler out here, so we can take care of the dog."

"Will it be destroyed?" she asked, with a funny mixture of hope and contrition.

"I doubt it." Mack had already dialed; he talked into the phone for a minute with his back turned, while the woman gazed at him with a puzzled frown.

He hung up. "There's just the one dog, check?"

"Well, yes, I think so. Of course, there used to be two, but I haven't seen the other one lately. I try not to see even this one *at all!* If only Emily had left an address –"

Mack had already opened the door and she followed us out onto her concrete back steps and stood with her arms clasped tightly against the cold, still talking.

"Thank you very much," Mack said. She smiled uncertainly and went back into the house, but closed only the storm door and stood inside it looking out at us through a spot wiped free of condensation. "What I'd like to do," Mack said in an almost inaudible whisper, "is ream my ears out, but not with her standing there. Sheesh, what a talker. You think she could be married?"

"She gushes, all right."

"Oil, and we'd be rich." The dog had been lying on the steps. It dragged itself to its feet and started growling again. "Come on, we'll wait in the car."

Mack slopped back down the drive with me at heel and we got into the Honda to wait. "Something I didn't tell you, J.J. We got the number from the phone company, and we tried to call, and no answer. So they got a technician out here to fiddle with the box on the pole, and he says no ringers are attached in the house. It's got lines for two, and he says none. What does that make you think of?"

"The phones in Hawley's car." Nobody can say I won't oblige an old friend.

"So now we know why Karen hasn't contacted you. No telephone. No coat, no shoes. Dangerous dog in the yard. And probably scared to death that the guy would just walk off with Joey, or worse, if he got back and found her not there, and that would be the end of it. But I'll tell you, all of this to keep a woman quiet – that suggests to me that he doesn't intend to harm her. So keep your chin up."

My chin was up, good and tight to keep my teeth from chattering.

"Here comes the dog man."

A dark blue wagon with a heavy wire screen between the front seat and the back pulled up to the curb in front of us, and a mild-looking, sad-eyed little man who reminded me of the Hush Puppy basset hound got out. Mack went to meet him. I tagged along. "Probably starving," I heard Mack say. "Or at least, not fed since Wednesday."

The guy dived back into the wagon and came out with a bag of doggie treats and a long gun. "Good thing school's in session," he said. "At least we don't have to fight off the kids."

The three of us scuffled back up the drive, to the gate where the dog still watched. "Skinny, all right," the dog man said. "Poor fella." He tossed a couple of doggie treats into the yard, just in front of the Doberman's feet. The dog glanced at them and stood his ground. "Pretty well trained," the dog man said. "You two stay where you are."

He backtracked down the drive a few steps. "Rattle the gate, okay, Mack? Watch your fingers."

Mack rattled the gate, and the dog sprang toward it. Mack stepped back, there was a muffled *fflutt* as the dog put his paws on the fence, and a dart flew into the animal's flank.

"Perfect," the dog man said. He came back up the drive. The dog gave Mack a worried look, nosed at its flank and knocked the dart loose, blinked, looked back at Mack, and began to lie down slowly. Mack reached for the gate.

"Not yet. It'll be a couple of minutes more before he's really out."

We stood quietly watching the dog. From inside the house came a thudding noise, three thuds close together, three far apart, three close together.

"She's in there!" I yelled. "Hang on, Kay, we're coming!"

"I wonder where this Michock woman really is?" Mack mused. "I can't picture her going away and only 'Africa' for a forwarding address."

The dog's head touched the ground and the body relaxed. "Let's cage him," the handler said. "I'll back the car up."

He trudged down the driveway muttering to himself and got into the wagon and backed it up the driveweay. "Okay," Mack said. "Now, if you brought the bolt cutters, we're all set."

The man glanced at him sad-eyed and rummaged in the front seat of the wagon until he found a tire iron. "Not much to that lock." He put the pry end of the iron into the hasp of the padlock, wrenched at it for about one second, and the hasp sprang open. Mack opened the gate and bent down to lift one end of the dog.

The second Doberman came flying around the corner of the house. "Look out!" I shouted. "There's another one!" Mack, still in a squat, twisted and brought his arm up to shield his throat from those long yellow teeth. He went down under the weight of the charge, and the dog, silent and determined, let go of his forearm and went after his throat. I punched it in the side of the head, knocking it sideways.

"Run," Mack gasped. The dog went for him again.

I got a hand in the choke chain and heaved backward with everything I had. That got the beast's attention. It turned and snapped at me, then went after Mack some more. I got hold of the end of the chain and pulled with my heels set, sliding across the mushy snow as Mack tried to scramble out of the way. Two more links of the collar slipped through the loop and the dog gagged. It took a good five seconds to black out, and for every one of them it was trying to get its teeth into Mack.

"Keep a little tension," the dog man said casually. He plunked another tranquilizer dart into the dog's flank. The other dog was already in the back of the wagon. Talk about cool! "Out, shut the gate," he said.

I stepped through the gate and shut it just as the dog groggily rammed its head against it.

"Brutal to those defenseless animals!" Emily Michock's friend was shrieking. "I'll call my councilman, I will, I'll call the minute City hall opens, I'll call the chief of police, you're going to be in big trouble, you dirty cops, you wait, I'm going to call –"

"Try Africa," I said. The two policemen paid no attention to the woman.

"Let's hope that's the last of them," the dog man said. "We must have caught this one napping." He and Mack lifted the second dog into the back of the wagon and slammed the gate.

"Killing two innocent animals! When all they were doing was protecting their own property! I'm going to call –"

"Do you believe this?" I asked Mack.

He shrugged. "You get used to it."

"My brother's sister-in-law plays bridge with the mayor's cousin! You'll hear about this! You –"

"Maybe Hawley should have yanked her phone while he was at it," I said.

"Stay cool," Mack advised.

"I got about twenty minutes before these two wake up," the dog man said. "You want to check out the yard?"

"Stay here," Mack said to me. He went into the yard with his hand on his gun, checked a doghouse beside the garage, disappeared on the other side of the house, came back from the front with his holster snapped. "That's got it," he said.

The door next door slammed mightily.

"You want these two in the pound?"

"Hang onto them, they could be evidence," Mack said. "Thanks."

He mounted the back steps of the house as the blue wagon moved down the drive. "This Emily likes her protection," he said. The black-and-blue eye of Operation ID stared back at us from one of the glass panels of the back door, and two bright brass locks protruded next to the jamb, the way deadbolt locks sometimes do.

"Going to break in?" I asked. The thudding inside had stopped.

"Not yet. Got to wait for the warrant." Mack sat on the wooden porch railing and looked out at the backyard. "Jeez, what a mess," he said. "Want to know why I don't own a dog?"

The far-off pounding had started again when two police officers arrived with the search warrant, fifteen minutes later. I'd walked around the house and yelled to Karen from the place where I thought the pounding sounded loudest, and the thuds had stopped for a while, then started again. I found the chain for the second dog attached to the fence on the other side of the yard, and a beaten-down trail leading to it from the front walk.

The cops were going through a charade of knocking on the door and announcing themselves when I came around the corner of the house. With Emily in Africa, she didn't hear; Hawley was in the hospital and no one could possible be left but Karen, who couldn't come to the door; I resented every second they waited for an answer.

"Keep him out of here, can't you?" one of them said to Mack. "He's too jumpy."

"He'll be all right."

"We go in first," the doubtful one said to me. "You got that?" He was a guy in his fifties with a little belly and a weathered face who reminded me of my father. I nodded.

"Any trouble, you go *out,*" he added. "Don't wait to be told, just get."

"He knows all that," Mack said. The third cop, a young guy with a fringe of blond hair that stuck straight out where his hat rested on it, was working on the door. He busted out a small pane of glass just over the locks, and it fell against the curtain and back out onto the porch. The cop tried to push the curtain aside. "I'm damned," he said. "There's a board in here."

"I'm going to report that you damaged Emily's house," shouted the woman next door. "You've got no right to break into her house! It's – it's breaking and entering, that's what it is!"

"Give me the section number," the young cop muttered. "I can't get this started. Got a tire iron?"

He worked at the door a few more minutes to get the board loose, reached inside, and pulled his hand out with an exasperated sigh. "Keyed inside, no keys," he reported.

"Basement window?" Mack asked.

"Boarded over, too," I said. "Every last one of them."

"Let's try the door again. Give it the old heave-ho," suggested the older cop.

He and Mack put their shoulders to the door and accomplished a lot of grunting. "Won't go," Mack gasped.

"What about the front door?"

The three of them glanced at me as if they'd forgotten my existence, which they probably had, and we trooped around to the front door. More knocking and identifying. "Better leverage, only one lock," the young cop said. "Try again?" He opened the storm door.

Mack examined the door. "Steel," he said. "We won't get far with that. Jeez, the place is a fortress. Anybody know Santa Claus real well?"

Nobody laughed. I set off on another foray

around the house while they conferred, this time looking as well as listening. Beside the chimney, one on each side, were small, high windows with shutters inside them. The storm windows fitted with turnbuttons. "Hey, here we go," I shouted.

The three cops came around the house and took a look at the windows. Inside, the pounding started again. "Looks good," Mack said. He pulled his pocketknife out and unfolded the screwdriver. "Here, J.J., you're the lightest, I'll give you a leg up." The other two traded glances but said nothing; even the young one outweighed me by a good thirty pounds.

Mack boosted and I clawed for the windowsill. I tried to rest as much weight on it as I could. Mack's built like his namesake vehicle and I might have been the lightest man around, but still I'm no sylph. The screws turned hard, rusted in place, and I could see I was going to have to pry through some paint to work the storm sash loose. It came suddenly, and my grab for it left Mack swaying on his feet.

"Don't do that to me, J.J. What you got?"

"Looks like the inside window pushes in. It must have a lock, but I don't see where."

"Up top?"

"I still don't . . . oh, it's hinged at the top.

Brace yourself." I leaned on one forearm and tried pounding the bottom of the window with the heel of my other hand. From inside the house came faint answering thuds. *We're coming, Karen,* I thought. The shutters inside drifted away from the glass, opening into a dark room. "I wonder why it's so dark?" I said. "Mack, I'll need a pry bar."

I got down and somebody went for a tire iron. This time it was Mack who climbed -up and the other two cops who held him. The window gave with a soft crunch. "Dry rot," Mack said. He pulled himself up and thrust one leg inside. "See you at the side door, folks," he said to the three of us outside. "Police," he yelled into the house.

Thump, thump, thump.

I followed the other two back around the house. The front door opened as we went past. "Here we go," Mack called. "Wait until you see this." I filed in after the cops.

"I can get you for breaking and entering, J.J.," Mack said cheerily.

"Don't joke."

Two-by-fours had been nailed to the walls beside each window, and over that, three-quarter-inch plywood. The draperies hung out the bottom of the covers and conducted a little light into the room, and between that and the open window by the fireplace there was enough illumination to show furniture shoved into a rough pile at one side of the room. I could see why the two little windows had been missed: with the shutters still closed, the mate to the pair looked solid, like paneling, and the wood had been painted to match the walls. Standing against the coat closet door were three two-by-fours that had barred the front door.

"Emily won't like this," Mack said.

The thumping came from downstairs. Mack stuck his head into the hall on the way through the dining room and gave the dark bedrooms a cursory glance. We walked into the kitchen as the younger cop was turning the last of four bolts on the basement door. The back door, too, had wooden bars across it. No wonder it wouldn't give.

The young cop flipped a light switch over the stairs. Nothing happened. "No lights," he announced, and pulled his flashlight off his belt.

"What are you doing here?" the big cop asked me. "Go sit in a chair." He pointed toward the kitchen table, a dim hulk in the bits of light that escaped the boarded windows.

"It's my wife we're looking for."

"Sit, I said."

I waited until the three of them were down

the stairs and started sneaking down myself. Mack had found the fuse box and he threw the one circuit breaker that showed a light. A couple of bare bulbs came on. "Thought so," he said.

A thump right beneath me made me jump "Under the stairs," I said. "A closet under the stairs!"

"You don't listen too good, do you?" asked the cop who had told me to take a seat, but he sounded amiable enough. He twisted a couple of plywood turnbuttons that held the closet door shut. Karen stumbled out. He put out his hands and caught her.

Mack stepped up and unknotted the gag. "Thanks," she croaked. I slipped off the side of the staircase and pulled her into my arms, almost in tears, but she couldn't return my hug, her hands were locked behind her in heavy handcuffs and her wrists were rubbed bloody.

"Oh, Karen," I said. "Oh, I promise, I'll get him for this."

"He's got Joey," she said thickly.

"No. Joey's fine, Joey's OK. I got him back night before last, he's just fine. Don't worry."

"He took him away two days ago, Joe." She worked her mouth for more words. "He never came back."

"Don't worry," I repeated. "Joey's just fine."

The others were trying keys in the handcuffs, but none fit. "Did she leave?" Karen asked. "I didn't hear her go, is she gone?"

"Wait, I'll try the knife." Mack opened something out of his red pocketknife and started sawing at one of the links that joined the cuffs. "We can get the chain apart, anyway."

"He never came back," Karen said.

"Hawley?"

"Is that his name? He kept taking Joey away and the telephones and I couldn't call even if she wasn't here and the windows are all boarded over and he showed me the dogs, he said if he came back and I wasn't here he'd throw Joey to the *dogs*, Joe, like the piece of meat.... Oh, God, he keeps them hungry and they're mean dogs, I..." She sobbed once.

"Hey, it's coming," Mack said.

"The dogs are gone," I soothed, rubbing Karen's back. "Hawley's in the hospital. Joey's there, too, but he's fine, we can go pick him up this morning."

"Is that what it is? Morning? I must have been in there all night, oh, I hated it, that rag in my mouth made me so thirsty and sick, and things kept crawling on me. . . .”

“Two nights, Karen. But he can’t do it ever again.”

“Cheap handcuffs,” said the big cop, rocking back on his heels with his thumbs in his back pockets.

“No, not him,” Karen said. “He never did anything like that. It was her, it was when he didn’t come back that she locked me in there!”

“She?”

“Emily,” Karen said impatiently. “Emily did it. This is Emily’s house!”

The door at the top of the stairs closed softly and I distinctly heard all four bolts turn home. A couple of wooden bars slid into place, and I realized what the metal loops I’d half-noticed beside the door must be for. Light footsteps crossed the floor, first into the living room and then back through the kitchen. The back door slammed.

“The driveway’s blocked,” the younger cop said. “She can’t get far.”

I had the feeling it didn’t much matter.

Chapter Fifteen

One of the links of the handcuffs finally gave, and Karen stretched her arms up and forward and sideways, bent her elbows, shrugged her shoulders, winced. "Thanks, Mack," she said. "Any longer and I'd have frozen that way."

"What's the smell?" asked the younger cop.

We all sniffed. "Kerosene," said the older one.

We looked at each other in anxious silence for a moment. The younger cop licked his upper lip and glanced at Mack. "She wouldn't torch her own house?" he said uncertainly.

"Oh, she would." Karen's mouth, with the red grooves pressed in her cheeks by the gag still like a perverted grin, was bitter. "Oh, our Emily would do absolutely anything. What is it, Friday? then she doesn't need the house anymore. Because tonight is the night Emily is going to be picked up by a flying saucer and spun away over the rainbow. She's planning to burn her car for a beacon, why not her house?"

"Burn it? Not sell it and burn the money?" I asked. "That's what the others were going to do."

"Damn it, Joe!" Karen exploded. "Couldn't you just this once have kept your nose out of whatever these crackpots were cooking up? Prue Watson says jump and you run out and buy a hoop! Just *once* –"

"Karen, I swear to you, Prue had nothing to do with this." Not the way she meant, anyway.

"Cool it," Mack snapped. "We got other problems."

The back door opened again and the light footsteps crossed the kitchen. "Forgot the matches," Karen said.

"Emily!" The lady from across the driveway, upstairs in the kitchen. I wondered if she'd gotten dressed. "Emily, when did you get back?"

"Hey!" the cops yelled.

"Emily, what's going on?"

"Hey!"

"Get out, Stella."

"Well, after all I worried and worried and was thinking I'd call you in Africa –"

"Hey!"

"– and that horrible man, and those dreadful dogs, what has he done to your windows?"

"Hey!"

"– and where's Mitzie? Who's that yelling?"

"Get out." Scuffling noises crossed the kitchen floor. Stella squealed for help.

"Hey up there!"

The door slammed and the voices, rising but indecipherable, continued in the yard.

"Your knife, Mack," Karen demanded.

"Karen, no way is that going to pry the wood off these windows," Mack said. "Half-inch plywood, and big nails –"

"Just give it to me." Mack handed her the knife and began to examine each of the windows, all identically nailed up and covered with plywood. Karen ran to the one corner of the cellar where there were no windows, on the other side of the stairs. I heard water run. "Somebody get the gas," she yelled.

The older cop had wrapped his ham-sized fist in his jacket and was pounding at the plywood of a window at the other end of the basement. Stupid, I thought. I looked around – never had I seen so empty a basement – and located the gray bulk of the gas meter.

A crackling noise started over my head as I yanked on the valve. Emily had started the fire in the living room, where all the furniture had been piled. Maybe she'd planned the fire for that night, everything going up in a blaze of glory, and all she'd had to do was pour the kerosene over it and touch it off. I remembered what Ferraro had said about purification by fire. Loonies, loonies.

I ran to try to help the big cop. A small explosion as I crossed the cellar rained dirt and tiny startled creatures out of the ceiling. He pounded harder at the plywood. Only one thin crack had appeared. I jammed my hands into my jacket pockets in despair and found the spoon I'd eaten the pineapple with, shoved the point of it under a corner of the plywood land pried. It was too short, bent at the wrong angle for leverage, and only the barest space appeared before it bent and broke.

Karen ran toward us with something in her hands I didn't recognize, a long piece of metal bent length-wise into a right angle, with flanges on one end. The handcuffs jingled as she thrust it at the big cop. He took it with a frown and pushed a flange under the corner I'd loosened, pulled the long end. "It's coming," he breathed. "It's coming," he shouted, as the crack widened. "It's coming!"

All of us crowded up to the window, Mack heaving at the corner of the plywood that had been started, the older cop levering frantically at the screeching nails. The board came free with a jerk that sent both of them staggering, and the third man and I jumped to open the window.

No one had ever expected to open that window. Not the last person to paint it, anyway. "It's stuck," the blond cop half-sobbed. "It's stuck."

Karen darted back into the basement corner. "Come back," I shouted. She said something I couldn't hear. The roar of flames was loud in the front corner of the house, smoke had begun to layer under the joists and creep downward.

"Here," Karen gasped, pressing something into my hand. Mack's knife, the screwdriver open. I got the blade into the crack at the bottom of the sash and started the window out. Someone got a purchase on the corner with the lever-thing Karen had found. The window bounced open.

"Hurry," someone muttered. Karen was lifting, Karen's head was out of the window, she reached out and her feet disappeared. The young cop stretched and hooked the window out of the way as the electricty fizzled and the lights died with a pop. Karen's hands and head reached back in, someone thrust me toward her, she grasped my arms and heaved. My belly scraped over the window frame. I scrambled out and reached back. The big cop now, Mack and the younger one lifting. Karen and I hauled him through the window, a tight fit that left him cursing. He pushed Karen out of the way, coughing, and reached down with me for the blond cop, an easy lift, and scuttled back.

"It's going to go," he said. "Get back." The young cop glanced from him to the window.

I leaned in for Mack, twining my arms with his, hoping he wouldn't pull me down. Someone grabbed my hips, and I shifted my grip until I had Mack under the arms and pulled, pulled, pulled, pulled, my sweaty cheek slipping against his while he tried to scale the smooth wall. His shoes slipped. For a moment his whole weight hung on my aching shoulders, and then he got a foot against the wall and boosted upward. He came over the sill already scrambling to get clear. There was a boom behind him and the cellar turned red.

"Sweet Jesus, Mary, and Joseph," he coughed, and got to his feet still coughing. "I don't mean you, J.J. No more like that! What was that thing you found, Karen?"

"Leg off the laundry tub."

"Move the cars," the big cop said. "Here comes the red truck."

Mack and the younger cop trotted across the front lawn, played after-you-Alphonse at the gate for a moment, jumped into their respective vehicles and drove them down the street a ways. The entire end of the house where the fire had started was burning now, the living room window complete with drapes and plywood lying across the foundation plants at a crazy angle. The smell of burning juniper and pine filled the air. Karen and I and the older cop kept to the fence as we made for the gate: next door, Stella what's-her-name, still in her flowered housecoat but with a down jacket thrown over it now, gave us a sour look and went back to playing a garden hose on the side of her house.

Mack and the other cop rejoined us on the sidewalk across the street. "I suppose you know none of this would have happened if we'd followed procedure?" the older man said. He coughed several times, bright red. "Or if your friend here had done what he was told?"

"J.J. does what he has to do," Mack said, not looking at either of us. "You want somebody sitting in the kitchen, you better do it yourself." My jaw sagged, and the other two cops moved slightly toward one another and away from Mack.

"Mack, I'm sorry," I said.

He gave me a funny look and went down the street to the Honda and got into it and drove away.

"It's my fault," Karen said. "I didn't know just how crazy she was, even though I knew she gave away her dog – I tried so hard to tell her that man was a phony, but she'd just get mad or go spooky on me... then when he didn't come back and didn't come back she blamed it on me, somehow. If I had had the run of the house, still –"

The two remaining policemen glanced at her and went a few steps farther down the sidewalk. "Joe," Karen said. "Did you bring the car? Because I've got no shoes."

I looked at the cops. They didn't look at me. I gave Karen my galoshes and borrowed a phone from a neighbor who had come out to look at the fire and called a cab and promised to meet it at the next intersection, because of the fire. By that time the street was crisscrossed with hoses and the pros had taken over from Stella what's-her-name, who had retreated loudly to a neighbor's porch.

It wasn't even nine o'clock.

Chapter Sixteen

Saturday. A day when Joey, with enchanting delight, and Karen, with mixed delight at being home and horror at my housekeeping habits, were rediscovering the house. A huge bundle of carnations had arrived that morning, with a card for Karen from Lars Pedersen. She had arranged them in two vases, with a dazed smile and tear-streaked cheeks. An hour later the doorbell rang again. "You'd better get that," I said. "It's probably more flowers."

Wrong. It was Mack.

Karen flung her arms around his neck and buried her face next to her left arm and hugged him tightly. I might have been jealous on another day, but that morning anything was fine with me. Within reason. Mack put his hands one on each side of her ribcage and squeezed tentatively, then pushed her gently away and came into the family room.

"I thought you'd like to know that Michock woman showed up at Hyland Lake last night, looking for her UFO. Bloomington took her in, but she's in the hospital now."

"Hurt?"

"Screaming nuts. If she's ever fit to stand trial, she'll be charged with five counts of attempted murder, something like false imprisonment, accessory after the fact of kidnapping, and a few other things. Nobody can get a straight story out of her, so who knows?

"She hasn't got a straight story," Karen said. "The woman gave away her dog, Mack. She'd had the mutt eight years! She'd been hiding in that house for weeks to purify herself of human contacts, all Hawley's idea. The fire was his, too."

Mack nodded. "Quite a guy. You think he had her hypnotized, something like that?"

"Not necessary, believe me." Karen shrugged. "She thought he was from another planet, what does that tell you? All because his eyes are a funny silver color."

"How come you went with him?" Mack asked, his face only mildly curious. One of my first questions, too.

"He had a gun on Joey. I didn't know it was empty. All I could think of was Mrs. Eskew and her Luger."

Mack was surprised by a yawn. "She's pretty impressive," he agreed. Mrs. Eskew had once shot a hole in my backdoor screen, but that's another story.

"Mrs. Eskew got Emily Michock's license number, by the way," I told Karen. "She remembered it because she was playing the game, and the word was *deliquesce.*"

"Pretty good." Karen looked out the back window at the patches of lawn the color of shredded wheat that had appeared over the past few days. "So that's what took you so long. I'll have to hear all about her trip."

Mack admired the flowers and told me how much Pedersen must have paid for them. Two of a kind, in a way, those two. Joey, who had been sitting on the floor doing a Consumer's Union wear test on one small segment of carpet with a toy truck, suddenly looked up. "Where's S'age?" he asked.

"Gone bye-bye," Karen said.

"Bye-bye, bye-bye," Joey repeated, going back to his wear test.

"You guys got any coffee?" Mack asked. "I'm about falling asleep, here. I only got four hours in yesterday afternoon."

"Oh, sure." Karen got up and set up some coffee, and we moved into the kitchen. The table looked funny without its oatmeal smear and its note. Karen had appreciated the note but not the smear, and I hadn't tried to explain it to her. Already, the whole thing was receding. Life was taking over.

"I got something to tell you, Karen," Mack said. He shot a glance at me. "And you stay out of it. I want you to know that you maybe had a bad week, but you ought to hear about the week J.J. had."

"Mack –"

"Stay out, I said." He looked at me a moment, and then he started to talk. He talked a long time. We had another pot of coffee, and then Mack looked at his watch and got up and stretched. "Well, I got to go protect society," he said. "Thank the lord I've got tomorrow off; I'm about bushed."

I saw him to the door and came back to sit again at the kitchen table with Karen. "Mack's a good guy," she said.

"None better."

"Oh, I don't know. There's you." She smiled and reached out and patted my hand. "I'm only sorry it took Mack to tell me how good."

"Just so long as you figure it out somehow," I said.

Epilogue

Three months later, the snow gone, Karen seized a sunny Saturday morning to plant some lettuce in her garden. She'd only been outside a minute or two when I saw her run across the backyard waving the newspaper she'd taken out to kneel on. I met her at the door.

"Joe," she gasped. "Look at this!"

I looked:

STING OPERATION ENDS

Los Angeles - AP. Police and FBI agents today ended a sting operation designed to discover industrial spies after what was termed a "very successful" run of one year. According to a spokesman for the Los Angeles Police Department, fifteen major cases of industrial espionage were uncovered. Operating as Arvel Ripov Associates, Inc. . . .